A DREAM

A DREAM

Ishan Dafaria

PARTRIDGE

A Penguin Random House Company

To order additional copies of this book, contact
Partridge India
000 800 10062 62
orders.india@partridgepublishing.com

www.partridgepublishing.com/india

ACKNOWLEDGMENTS

THIS BOOK WOULD NOT HAVE been without the help of Ms. Mubeena Rehman, my friend, philosopher and guide throughout the journey of this book.

Also, it goes without saying, a Big thanks to mummy (Smt. Sunita Dafaria) and papa (Dr. Pinkesh Dafaria), for their unconditional love and support.

And finally, to some of my friends and teachers and all those people, who taught me so much in my life and directly or indirectly contributed towards the making of this book.

PROLOGUE

June, 2012, Cape Verde, West coast of Africa.

SHE SWITCHED OFF THE 80" plasma TV and sighed. Turning back slowly, she looked at the large beautiful solid gold wall clock that hung on the wall behind her. It was almost 11'o clock.

She got up and walked up the staircase to the first floor where there were two rooms to the right and one master bedroom to the left. The walls were as richly decorated as they were on the ground floor, with all the exquisite paintings and wall designs. She checked in on the first room on the right which was a study. There was nobody there. She turned back and looked in the master bedroom and there he was . . . sitting on the bed, probably lost in some other world . . . with his laptop in his lap, working, which according to her was totally irrelevant. "Baby, you done with work?"

"I don't' know. I just don't feel like sleeping." He answered without even looking up. His voice was hoarse with emotion. Even in the dim lights she could see the lines of tension on his forehead. "The past isn't easy to forget. Especially when you have lost everything that you cared about just to gain that perfect dream life." She said.

"I understand you are upset. But that's why I am here for." She said in the most seductive tone that the typical Indian women could afford.

He looked up at her to say that he wasn't in a mood for romance. But then he saw her, under the yellow light . . . wearing that hot Agent Provocateur lingerie that did so little to hide the curves of her young body.

He sighed, he so much wanted to be with her, but the sight of 5 bullets being fired in the chest of his best friend was not leaving his mind. She looked down as she realized that her attempt to take his mind off had failed. The political battle that her husband had to fight to achieve this dream . . . the friends that were closer to them than their families . . . their own, REAL identities . . . that are now dead according to the records . . . all that they lost and all that learnt was just a dream for her . . . She neither remembered the new villa he had bought. The richness and the grandeur of their new lives, the esthetic paintings that adorned the wall . . . something they could not afford back in India. He was not one of those men who went cold due to stress of work or age or differences between married couples. He was at a totally different loss. His problem was . . . he got what he wanted . . . the perfect dream life . . . utopia . . . a silent country, a huge villa by the beach, a career as a writer, assets, properties and Swiss bank accounts adding up to almost 12000 crores of Indian currency and the most loving wife anyone could have . . . but it all came with a price . . . A really bad deal . . . . A bargain with life . . . where he lost more than he could afford . . . The loss of his country and everything that meant to him . . . his friends, his relatives, his country, his people . . . . His identity.

He got up and smiled . . . Every single memory was crashing in his mind again and again . . . She eyed him sleepily as she moved to the bed, as she tried to put all these thoughts away . . . sex definitely had the power to make your heart smile in any situation your mind was in.

"Where are you going Adhir? Come let's sleep."

He saw her big, beautiful eyes. They were deep, you could lose yourself in them if you had a thing for pure and flawless beauty, untainted and untouched . . . . He picked up the glass of wine resting on the side table and gulped down a mouthful and looked back at her. With a slight smile which she could easily tell was fake, all he said was "I am no longer Adhir, I am Ranvijay." Saying so he pulled out a cigar from the night stand and slowly walked out into the porch taking long slow drags with his head bent low . . . .

CHAPTER 1

January, 2012. New Delhi, India.

HE SAT ON THE CHAIR as he thought about the conversation he had with his wife . . .

"We are not going to Delhi, Prithvi."

"Of course we are."

"Prithvi, Delhi is the heart of Indian politics. And Indian politics has crime and corruption in its very soul."

"I know and that's why I want to go there."

"Are you even listening to yourself? Do you know how many honest lives have been ruined by politics? You are a man of fine intellect. Why don't you consider all the pros and cons???"

"I am thinking about everything dear. I've always wanted to improve the Indian system of administration. And now that I am getting a chance you are saying that I should drop it???"

"I know that you really want it . . . but Prithvi . . . we should know our limits . . . it's not anywhere near easy for an honest man to survive in politics, much less improve it."

"Why don't you understand??? It's something that I have wanted to do forever in my life . . . Making India corruption free . . . Make it a more peaceful and a happier place to live in . . . ."

"I know your intentions are good . . . but the thing that you want to achieve is not possible for one person. You need a whole group of able masterminds to fight it . . ."

"So what do you want? I sit here and watch some bastards ruin my country? Is that what you want, to see our country being left in the hands of some ruthless selfish people who work for their own selfish motives??"

"No honey, I too want our country to be better . . . . but not by risking your life. What you want might take a serious toll on you and you may end up somewhere you never wanted to be. At the end, even if you survive you will be left with no one and also a corrupt country. You will have only yourself to blame. Nothing matters to me as much as you . . ."

"Oh common Avni, it's the same for me. You matter the most to me. But at the same time it's about something that I have wanted all along. This was the very reason I joined the forces. But Jaipur is a quiet place. I really can't do much from here. If you really want to see me happy . . . then come with me to Delhi . . ."

"I know but . . . leave it . . . I know how much this means to you and no argument on Earth would make you stay. You know your dreams matter to me as much as they matter to you. But still . . . . All I can say is think once more. Will you?"

"Ok I will think . . ."

The whole conversation from the last week was still ringing in his ears . . . . He hadn't given much of a thought to it then, but now, sitting in his cabin in New Delhi, he was thinking about it. He knew somewhere Avni was totally correct, and may be in some parallel universe he would have listened to her reason, but here he was. Mixed feelings, looking intently at the wooden table in front of him, his mind lost in the thoughts of his wife and the life changing decision he made 6 days ago.

Suddenly there was a knock on his cabin's door that stirred him out of his thoughts. "Come in" he responded, sitting up straight from the comfortable position. It was the sub-inspector Randhir Singh.

"Welcome to Delhi, Sir. Sub-inspector Randhir Singh reporting, Sir." He said as his right hand raised in the saluting manner and his lips curved in the formal smile and a strained expression which Prithvi recognized almost immediately.

"On behalf of Vatsalya Police station, I welcome you. I thought if you would like I'd explain you a little about the areas we cover and introduce you to the other policemen in the police station. Prithvi noticed the over used uniform and the fact that though the sub-inspector didn't look very old by his face, his hair had stated greying over the ear. Unlike Jaipur, where the policemen seemed a lot more relaxed and happy, here policemen looked over-exerted. 'Stress and hard work I suppose. Welcome to Delhi Prithvi' he thought to himself as he followed the policeman.

"Sir, after this we have to go to the Ramleela Maidan. There is a press conference with the Bharat Jan-Hit party next week, so we two have to be there as the DIG sir will go over the security plan." the sub-inspector added as they exited his cabin.

. . . .

Same time, same city, different place.

'Another day with these idiots. My life is getting wasted. Can't figure out a way to live a proper satisfactory life. And now to top it off, the people want answers. I seriously need to figure a way out of here as fast as I can.' Thinking thus Adhiraj Goswamy got down from his white ambassador which was similar to everything in the country, outdated and exploited. People were gaining awareness about the black money because of some revolutionaries that were holding strikes in masses . . . . Everything was so calm an year ago and suddenly a rush of awareness had filled the public with rage . . . Although Adhiraj was somewhere happy because he wanted corruption to end but even he knew that this thing will never yield results . . . 'It's very hard to deal with politicians . . . they are the crankiest minds in the country and for how long will people drop their regular lives and keep on demonstrating on streets . . . . nobody gives a damn for long if they die during their protests or anything else happens . . . This was the major problem . . . . The desired outcome was good . . . no doubt . . . it was terrific . . . but the means used were equally useless . . . It's true that through these ways only, we achieved great success in the past . . . the glorious history of India is full of such examples where nonviolence and patience has helped out. But today is a totally different day. This was a major problem . . . people think abstention from food for a few days will solve all the problems . . . And the general public is like a young kid . . . innocuous and avid . . . When they don't see their efforts bearing fruits, they pull back immediately . . . The revolutionary loses support and politicians in power use legal forces to make sure that the man is set down and does not take any steps against the government . . . and the chapter closes . . . People come out on the streets once again to say something good for the man, pay him a small tribute in the form of a silence and that's it . . . they get back to their usual routine . . . and everything comes back to where it started.

"Sir, water??"

Adhiraj came back to the real world . . . "Yes, thanks," he said picking up the glass of water . . . "So finally all the media is here??" He enquired as his sharp eyes scrolled around the room to have a glance of everyone present in the room . . .

"Yes I think so" Replied Aranya Dixit, the spokesperson, as he got up to take his place behind the mike "Soon I will be fired with a stream of questions for which I have no proper answers . . . ." he grumbled.

"Have a good time man . . . . you enjoyed a lot . . . now it's time for a pay-up" Adhiraj smiled as he too got ready for the questions that were to come in his plate . . . though he wasn't very honest and didn't do the work he should have been doing, he still did a better job than most of his colleagues . . . But, after all, he was a politician and the scams and crimes his party was accused of were somewhere true. Now, the strategy implied stalling them and buying enough time for themselves till most of the fire went down and they found answers for the remaining sparks.'

He had, somehow, accepted it . . . this life . . . It was his choice . . . wasn't it??? Every man is nothing but the result of his choices in the past . . . The so called luck and circumstances are just excuses for the terrible decisions in the past life . . . he chose to be a politician . . . and now he was paying the consequences . . . . A bad choice . . . he thought . . . .

. . . .

Same time, different city.

"Good afternoon ladies and gentlemen, welcome aboard. Thank you for travelling with us, we wish you a very happy journey. I am Kiran and me and my staff has got the opportunity to take care of you. Please press the light switch over head in case you need anything. Thank you." the gorgeous airhostess announced on the mic with a smile. Daksh was a very happy man today . . . he had seen his childhood friend Adhiraj in an interview on the national TV and realized that Adhiraj had finally made it through the long ladder in politics to the center . . . Daksh had decided then and there to give him a surprise visit as soon as possible . . . And then, a couple of months later he got a job opportunity in Delhi . . . He knew the job wasn't as good and tense free like the one he had in Bhopal but he loved to strip the corrupt ministers . . . he had created many enemies but he still fearlessly continued his job and now he decided to go to Delhi . . . . the central government . . . he wanted to go big . . . . his dreams and aspirations of being an awarded and internationally recognized journalist was driving him . . . . and he saw only one path to that destination . . . uncovering the faces of people who were ruining the country. He would go to any limits to do what he needed to in order to climb the ladder of success. 'Even if it means exposing Adhiraj . . .' he smiled devilishly . . .

"What are you thinking sweetheart??" Charvi's voice interrupted his thoughts . . . .

"I was thinking when I will finally become a father??" he said kissing Charvi's hand. She slapped him lovingly on the back of his hand and then they both grinned, Charvi shyly looking down and, "when you finally have time to raise a family". She then rested her head against his shoulder and they went into a deep relaxing sleep . . . . "Oh god . . . . you run fast", Adhiraj blurted out as he fell on his knees panting heavily in front of the small but beautiful house.

Prithvi turned around and saw his friend and laughed. Adhiraj looked up at him, he had grown immensely tall and strong in his late teens and now stood at almost 6 feet at the age of 18, broad shoulders and a dark complexion while he was just 5'6 and hadn't even started getting proper hair on his face.

Prithvi offered a hand to his friend and helped him get up. Soon Charvi and Daksh came easily strolling behind.

"It looks like Adhir lost again." Charvi teased him as she usually did whenever he lost a race to Prithvi.

"Why do you always keep coming after me?" Adhir scoffed as he glared at her.

"Maybe because you are the only one who is shorter and skinnier than her." Daksh too joined in as he and Charvi laughed and gave a high five to each other.

Adhiraj looked at Daksh for a moment and smiled. Daksh and Prithvi recognized this look and soon started apologizing. Charvi being the new one in the group didn't realize what was happening. She questioningly looked at Prithvi.

"Oh it's just that whenever we tease Adhir too much for his poor grades or short height or skinny physique, he gets some evil prank cooking in that brain of his." Prithvi explained.

Charvi looked at Adhir who was now grinning.

"He maybe lean and thin, but he is really very sharp when it comes to pranks or talking. You know in the past 8 years of us being together, he has got scolded for anything. He always finds a way out of every situation and either one of us or both of us end up in trouble." He said pointing at Prithvi and himself.

"By the way, what are you good at? Daksh is good at studies, and trust me, he has a great sense of humor. You say Adhir is a little evil genius. What about you?" Charvi looked at Prithvi.

"Oh he is good for nothing." Adhir joined in the conversation as he patted his friend's large back."

"Yeah . . . . He is good for nothing." Daksh joined in grinning.

"Well thank you friends . . . by the way . . . I am the athletics champion and also the class topper . . . ." Prithvi replied with a proud smile and a buffed up chest.

"And yes friends . . . Charvi here, is also very smart, extremely beautiful and has a smile that can drive anybody crazy . . ." Daksh replied placing an arm around Charvi's shoulder.

"Stop it . . ." she laughed and removed his hand.

"We have been best friends since we were 10. And now, sadly after 8 years, we have to go to different parts of the country for our careers", Prithvi continued.

"How can you live without your parents? I can't even think of doing that." Charvi said. "I mean, the day I heard my dad had to shift to Indore for business purposes, I started mentally preparing to move myself along with them. My father wanted me to stay there and complete my 12th, but I literally cried until mumma didn't agree to stay back with me."

"Umm . . . maybe because we are not childish girls who want to hug there teddies while sleeping." Daksh said and all the three guys burst out laughing.

Charvi looked in anger for a moment and then punched Daksh's back hard.

"Shut up ok. I am not childish. I just love my mumma and papa very much." Charvi glared.

"*Beta, come in. It's getting late.*" Charvi's mother came out in the veranda of her house to call her.

"*Haan mumma . . . aa rahi hu* . . . Okay guys . . . it was nice meeting all three of you. The last two days were awesome. Hope we meet again soon." So saying Charvi started walking back to her house.

"Hey Charvi . . . after these two go tomorrow, want go out for a coffee or something. There is this nice restaurant just at the corner. I have heard its pretty good."

"Ummm okay . . . why not? Sure . . ."

"It's done then . . . I'll see you tomorrow. Byeee . . ."

"Bye Daksh . . ." she smiled and turned back.

"Dude your new neighbor is hot." Daksh told Adhir as he watched her go.

"Dude don't even think about it. She is way above your league." Prithvi grinned as he placed a hand on Adhir's shoulder.

"Why so?"

"Well for starters . . . she is dumb . . . and secondly . . . she is the only daughter of a man who is a co-owner of a very reputed hotel chain . . . that means he is rich enough to buy her any kind of husband or boyfriend she likes . . ."

"Hmmm . . . . let's see . . . ." Daksh smiled.

"Let's go . . . it's really getting late now . . . ." Daksh said as Charvi disappeared inside.

"Hey common let's have a stroll together. We all part tomorrow. If you remember." Adhir said as he and Prithvi started towards the garden. Daksh looked back and then ran up to catch his friends . . .'

"Wake up Daksh, we have reached Delhi" he heard the sweet voice of his wife penetrating his dream. He glanced around with eyes half open and smiled as the last memory he had with his friends came back to him.

CHAPTER 2

A week later, Ramleela Maidan.

HIS SHARP EYES SCROLLED AROUND the garden for anything that might seem unusual or out of place. His eyes stopped upon one face that seemed oddly familiar . . . He pressured his brain for a couple of moments and then he realized . . . . this was Daksh. He couldn't believe his luck that his childhood friend was standing in the queue along with the other journalists waiting for the security check to get in the conference. All the past memories flooded him at once as he tried to contain himself with his emotions. He didn't know what to say . . . after a couple of moments of composing himself, he immediately called a policeman and asked him to get Daksh out of the security check and get him straight to him. The policeman did as he was told. He approached Daksh and asked him to accompany to the Senior Inspector. Daksh was reluctant but he had no choice . . . . He wondered as to what might have happened. The policeman took him inside from a side door without any security check straight to the police officers room, Daksh was confronted by a huge dark complexioned guy . . . who was at least 6 feet tall, weighing around 90 kilograms and a very wide grin on the face that had a large moustache . . . it took a moment before Daksh recognized Prithvi but in a matter of moments Daksh hugged him saying . . .

"*Arey bhai kaisa hai??? Kahan tha bhai???*"

"*Mai bdiya hu tu bata . . . Tu toh journalist ban gaya yaar . . .*"

"*Haan yaar . . . aur tu, bahut bada police officer . . .*"

"*Kahan yaar . . . bahut kharaab job hai . . . Anyways . . . you know Adhiraj will be here too . . .*"

"Haan bhai pata hai . . . soch raha tha press conference ke baad mil lunga . . ."

"Chal okay . . . Come here only . . . Saath me chal chalenge . . ."

"Okay done . . . ye mera card rakh le . . . ek call kr dena mujhe . . ."

Prithvi kept the card in his trouser pocket and smiled. Then he signaled the constable to escort Daksh and returned to his work.

Daksh smiled while walking back. This was a pleasant surprise. Maybe . . . just maybe . . . he could use Prithvi's post and power along with Adhiraj's to rescue himself or rise up . . . But now, turning attention to the job at hand. The interview that was to begin in the next half an hour. The notes he needed to make, the few specific questions he had for a couple of ministers, the general questions he had for the party, the notes, the reactions and etc. etc.

. . . .

After the conference, Bharat Jan-hit party, party office.

'Finally the conference is over', thought Adhiraj,' I seriously need some rest this chaos is starting to get on my nerves, my life is becoming sick' he thought as he laid back in his chair. 'These guys won't be able to achieve anything except giving us a hard time. Eventually it will get over and then everybody will lurk into darkness.' He thought as a smile came across his face. As a politician he loved challenges and this was the time when they were facing a really good challenge. He wondered why the opposition party hadn't joined in the movement. The movement was against the ruling party, not against the opposition. They would love to join in and overthrow the ruling party as soon as they can. Anyways . . . there's no sense in making any wild guess . . . they will do what they have to do . . . Everything has a logical explanation and many different point of views . . . we will deal with whatever comes our way . . .

"Knock knock" the sound of the door knocking drifted him out of the partial sleepy state.

"Who is it???" He stirred opening his eyes adjusting, them back to the sunlight coming directly in his room.

"Sir a police inspector and a news reporter wants to meet you, they say they are your friends" came in the doorman . . . .

"I don't have any friends in the news agency or police department. At least not yet." He smiled sitting up in his chair. "Check their IDs and send them in" he said wondering what a policeman and a reporter would want from him . . . soon his question was answered as the two friends came in with ear to ear grin and stood in front of Adhiraj. Adhiraj looked confused at the over friendly gesture of these two men who clearly didn't care about any sort of formality. They seem strangely familiar, he thought He studied them from top to bottom. The policemen was a tall and athletic guy. Standing around 6 feet tall. Still in the khaki uniform . . . The skin tanned from a lot of exposure to the sun. A hard face with a moustache . . . the reporter looked smarter and more confident of the two, clean shave . . . fair complexion . . . smart hairstyle . . . unusual for a guy in his late twenties . . . dressed in a slim fit formal shirt and blue denims . . . standing around 3 inches shorter than the policeman. "Didn't I tell you dude, this short heighted son of a bitch has a very bad memory when it comes to old friends. Common Adhir, don't you recognize your father?" There was only one guy who talked to him this way. It cannot be . . . . "Daksh . . . and Prithvi . . ." Adhiraj blurted in disbelief. He looked up to the two guys and almost jumped out of his chair . . . moving from the side of the large teak table and hugged the two friends one by one. Adhiraj couldn't believe this and for a moment felt this was a dream. After such a long time he had met people that could be called friends . . . because politics didn't give him the luxury of friends or much of a nice happy family . . . and these two were not just friends . . . these guys were more of a family to him . . . a lot more than his father ever was. The memories of his childhood where his own father hated him and these two supported him . . . The thought made his throat choke and he put his hands in his pocket and looked down and then back to them and smiled slightly but his eyes . . . they were flooding with every emotion a human anatomy could afford . . .

"Come on . . . have a seat." Adhiraj retreated back to his chair and motioned them to sit in front of him. The emotions were still there, the air was filled with a warm happiness. Daksh looked at Adhiraj's table and saw the same majestic wooden pen stand that Adhiraj's father used to have on his study table or his shirt pocket.

"He gifted it to me." Adhiraj answered realizing the question.

"Oh I thought he loved the pen a lot more than you."

"Well as a matter of fact he did . . . this pen meant nothing but pure excellence to him . . . but then . . . when he was on his death bed 6 years ago . . . he gave it to me . . . saying, and I quote . . . 'you never gave me any reason to be happy or proud . . . and I believed that you will live off my pieces for the rest of your life . . . but now since you have a career . . .

though the word career is an exaggeration when it comes to politics and politicians . . . still you have something . . . and so I give it to you . . . as a memoir . . . keep it safe . . .' and saying thus he passed away . . . mother died soon after . . . though I still believe he gave me this only because he didn't want it to go in any stranger's hands . . . anyway, I got it . . . and here it is . . . the only memory of my father . . ."

"I am really sorry bro . . . didn't intend to touch your nerve there . . ."

"It's okay . . . So how did you two come here all of a sudden??" enquired Adhiraj as he overcame his emotions and gained his composure.

Daksh then narrated the whole story to him.

"Ohhkkay . . . . Well this is amazing . . . . Having you guys here, reviving the whole friendship thing. Life ahead seems good." Adhiraj smiled.

"By the way we are all meeting tonight at my new place for dinner so both of you are cordially invited with your families. It will just be us and our families, so no formalities, no excuses, just be there on time," announced Daksh.

"Okay . . . I am in . . . 'said both the friends together . . .

"By the way . . . you remember Charvi?"

"Yes . . . don't tell me she is in Delhi too . . ." Adhiraj laughed.

"Well she is . . . as a matter of fact . . . I married her buddy . . ."

"Son of a bitch . . ." Prithvi was stunned.

"Are you serious?? I mean you ACTUALLY married Charvi . . . ." Prithvi looked at Daksh. "So when you said you like her you were serious??" Adhiraj sat up in his chair.

"Yeah man . . . I was serious"

"How in the world did that happen?" Adhiraj knew the taste and class Charvi's family preferred. And Daksh was nowhere near that.

"You know what they say . . . There's no girl who won't fall for Daksh's charms . . . and after all . . . a girl is a girl . . . and every girl, more or less is the same inside . . ."

'Honestly . . . aaj tak aisi koi bhi ladki hai jo tujhse na pati ho??"

'Sanjana ma'am yaad hai??'

"You mean the hot Sanjana ma'am . . . math teacher???"

"Haan . . . I tried on her a lot . . . but she always smiled and turned me down . . ."

"Saale . . ." Adhiraj looked at him with a smile and a little jealousy in his eyes.

"Hahaha . . . Well we'll discuss that later. Okay? I've got work to do, got to report at the office and then I will have to help Charvi in preparing the house a bit . . . we just moved last week so its still a bit messy . . . alright so . . . bye for now . . . I'll see you all today evening. Till then take care guys . . . ." So saying Daksh shook hands with the two friends and departed.

"Well man it's time for me as well. I'll come to your place first and then we will move together." Prithvi said as he too got up to leave.

"Okay, done." Adhiraj sighed as he saw his friend exit his cabin. The emotions were no more visible in his eyes . . . they were somewhere in his heart though . . . a couple of things came in his mind . . . but he discarded them . . . 'Common man . . . you should not use them as your stepping stones . . . they are your friends . . .' he said to himself as he got back to his chair.

. . . .

9:00 p.m., Outside Adhiraj's mansion.

Grrrrr . . . . The sound of Prithvi's jeep stirred the calm night outside the minister's mansion. Prithvi got out of the car and rang the door bell. A young woman, apparently Adhiraj's wife opened the door. Prithvi looked at her, she was extremely beautiful, sharp features, and a smile on the face, she greeted him. She wasn't very tall though. 'A perfect match for Adhiraj,' Prithvi smiled.

"Hello how can I help you?"

"I am Prithvi Raj Chauhan and this is my wife Avni, we are friends of Adhiraj's . . . and you must be Anjali . . . Right?"

"Yeah . . . Hi, Adhir told me about you. Come in. Have a seat. He would be back any moment. He wasn't supposed to go but he received a call in the evening asking him to report immediately." She smiled. As soon as she finished, there was opening of gates as Adhiraj's Mercedes rolled in. "There he is", she smiled.

The Mercedes stopped in the driveway behind the jeep and Adhiraj came out of the back seat, excited enough not to wait for the driver to open his gate, with his usual stature, hands joined in a formal Namaste and a smile for everyone. "Hey Prithvi . . . . Sorry I had to go for an emergency meeting. You know the circumstances these days . . . Everything is messed up and we people don't have a moment of peace . . . ."

"This is the reason why we work don't we? TO give hard time to corrupt guys . . ." Prithvi grinned.

Daksh grinned in return "I guess you have met Anjali, my wife," he said walking up to her and placing an arm around her shoulder.

"Yeah I have . . . ." Said Prithvi smiling. "Well this is Avni, my wife." He said placing an arm around her. A medium heighted woman, dressed in a red beautiful sari came a step ahead and greeted the couple folding her hands in the traditional Indian style. "Namaste." She smiled. 'A typical Indian woman in her late twenties, decent, shy and well mannered.' thought Adhiraj as he smiled and replied to her greeting. "What are you thinking dude. Ask us in." Prithvi broke in between. They all laughed and walked into the house. Adhiraj excused himself and went up the stairs in the hall.

Prithvi saw his trail and as he disappeared and then noticed the rest of the house. The house was two stories, must have been at least 16,000 sq. ft. he had guessed when he entered the premises, the stairs to the top floor besides the opening of the hall in the rest of the house which had a white curtain draped over it, barring his vision of the rest of the house . . . a large painting of a very beautiful girl with a life like red rose in her hand adorned the wall opposite to him, yellow lamps added to the aura of the room and a vase at least 5 ft. in height filled with artificial flowers was kept on the side adjoining the black leather sofas . . . the room was pure elegant white in color and the thing that amazed him most was that there was no ceiling fan . . . just central air conditioning . . .

"So how's life Anjali??" asked Avni to broke the awkward silence.

"Life's good. Just tensed up a bit due to the recent events in politics you know."

"Hahaha . . . yeah I understand. For a politician and his family, these kind of times aren't easy."

"Yes . . . he is mostly lost in himself these days . . . *Abhi tum dono se milkar* I saw him smiling after almost 6 months . . . what about you guys? How are you finding Delhi?"

"Delhi is good. A really big city compared to what we are used to living in. Hope we adjust soon." Prithvi said with a slight smirk on his face.

And the general talk continued for a while.

What's the discussion about guys?" Adhiraj asked walking down the stairs.

"Just asking your childhood secrets." Replied Anjali with a wink.

"Yeah as if I am the only one with dirty teenage secrets and a wife in this room." Replied Adhiraj as he smiled and took a glass of water from the table.

"Everybody keeps quiet. That was the promise bro." Prithvi looked at Adhiraj.

"Hahaha yeah . . . but out of all the three, Daksh has to worry the most about teenage secrets coming out . . .

"Hahaha yeah right . . . so let's go shall we?"

"Yes . . . off to Daksh's . . . ."

. . . .

CHAPTER 3

10:15 p.m., Daksh's house.

THE LOUD HORN AT THE door prompted many street dogs and night animals to stir and bark and chirp. Daksh and Charvi soon came out of their house to open the main door. Daksh opened the door, "Welcome everybody to Casa de Daksh."

"You still got that thing for foreign languages don't you???" Adhiraj smiled.

"Yes baby . . . Now I am learning Spanish. Kind of a hobby you know." Daksh replied as he hugged Adhiraj and then Prithvi.

"Oh my god. Is that big grown up beautiful girl in a jeans and a top Charvi? You still are wearing the same kind of clothes you used to wear 10 years ago." Adhiraj smiled.

"Yup and you are also standing at the same height you were standing 10 years ago." Charvi moved forward and hugged him. Daksh was taken aback for a moment at the extremely warm gesture. Then he happily responded with an effusive hug.

The laughing and chit chat continued as they moved inside the house.

Adhiraj being a keen observant didn't miss the luxury and taste in the house.

'This house, these walls, these paintings, flower vases, plasma TV . . . I didn't know honest reporters made so much money. And his parents weren't this rich either.' He looked at Charvi and thought her as the probable reason of this richness. 'She was rich, maybe that's why . . .' He just waved the thought away and made himself comfortable on the couch with others.

'So Charvi? How's life?" Prithvi broke the ice.

"Life is boring dude. Daksh goes out in the morning and doesn't come back till late evening. He hardly has time during the day. And well nights . . . you know most of the time he is too tired and sleeps off early." Everybody laughed.

"That's the story of most of the men you know." Anjali replied.

"Ummm . . . Baby I know we are all close friends and open with each other but I don't think this is something you say to anyone when they come to your house for the first time." Saying Daksh gulped down some wine.

"Well to be honest I think you women should carry the discussion somewhere else or not discuss at all." Adhiraj retorted. "It's not like we guys don't like any sort of spice in our marriages but after whole day of work anybody has the right to seek rest. And who do we earn for? You guys. You shop you eat you have fun . . . for that we work hard all day."

"Very correct bro. I am with you." Prithvi replied as he sipped his whiskey.

Daksh looked at the expressions of three women and intervened . . . "Ladies I think you should go in the bedroom. Why don't you show them all the things we bought for you baby? The new dresses and all that stuff."

Charvi nodded and took them to their bedroom.

And so the catching up of past 12 years of their life continued . . .

. . . .

Soon from the usual chitchat, they moved for dinner and the conversation turned . . . "Why did you guys come to Delhi?? The political situation will not allow the two of you to have a peaceful life." Adhiraj started.

"See my explanation is simple. I want to improve our country. It can't go on like this. You know Adhiraj, no offence to you, but the current politicians and situations, the Indian politics has a very indefinite and insecure future. What about the coming years??? The way it is going down . . . It can't go on like this. Someone will have to take the initiative, isn't it???" Prithvi said.

Adhiraj nodded and looked at Daksh.

"Same thing buddy. Even I was thinking something similar. You see with the scams and political affairs, everything is becoming uncertain. And I tried but it is impossible to improve the country from where I was.

There is no option but to rise at the national level and do something. And to be perfectly honest, I don't do this job for the betterment of the country, I actually do it for my self-satisfaction. I love this job. And I got bored at the state level . . ."

"But what you all are thinking is not possible here. The central scams are a lot more treacherous than they seem. Politics is not a bed of roses. You can't just play and win. It's really very difficult. And even if you win, it comes with a price. The deeper you go, the more you lose. And the more you lose, the lesser are your chances to win. It's impossible to end up corruption in this country . . . . And especially you Daksh, it's not skydiving . . . it's bloody national politics. Even I thought that I would improve the country by being an honest politician, but trust me . . . A simple and honest man's life becomes hell." Adhiraj countered.

"C'mon Adhiraj don't be a jerk. With the kind of 'team' that we are, nothing can stop us. All we need is a cool mindset and an effective working plan. That's all. And also, you are a part of the central government. You will help us I know. Its simple guys. We know all their secrets, they don't know ours. It'll be fun" Prithvi argued.

"Are you even listening to yourself . . . It's not going to be fun . . . grow up Prithvi. I'll tell you something. You know I was never interested in studies. Why do you think of all the possible line of occupations that my rich father could afford, I chose politics?"

Prithvi nodded.

"'It was because 8 years ago, I had a similar mindset as you do. In fact, a lot greater will than you have. Listen, I wasn't good in studies, but it was not because I couldn't perform well, it was because I didn't want to. I couldn't be a book worm like you guys. I always wanted to do something bigger, better, and more productive than just cramming and passing the exams. Life is a lot more than just passing an exam and getting a job. I wanted to do something larger. I thought and thought and thought . . . I was sick of the conventional methods and jobs so I decided to do something impossible. I decided to do something that would for once, make me and my father proud of myself . . . I joined politics . . . to change the system. It's not that I didn't try my best. I did. I gave in everything. But it just doesn't happen. It came to a point where my family started to get in danger and so I had to stop." Adhiraj said with almost anger in his voice.

"What's wrong guys??" Charvi and other women came in.

"Nothing . . . It's just I lost my temper." Adhiraj sat back in the sofa.

"It's a rare sight." Anjali put her arm around his shoulder.

"I agree . . . I never saw him angry, you have changed bro." Prithvi nodded.

"I haven't changed. It's just that the stress level is too high. I mean, every man is an artisan of his own fortune . . . I believe that, but somehow I failed. I couldn't achieve what I wanted to. And I don't want you two to hurt in the process." Adhiraj looked down.

"Hey baby common now don't be upset. I know you tried your best. But some things just aren't under our control." Anjali consoled him.

"Well I think Adhiraj is right. I mean what he said cannot be ignored. There is no guarantee of success and even if it comes, it would come with a real price." said Avni for the first time.

"The political scenario in India is very dirty. You two should not mess up your lives. Adhiraj is the most cool and collected guy I have seen in my whole life . . . and if it can mess up his life . . . I think you two should consider your choices . . . What is done is done . . . it can't be reversed." Anjali came in.

"Alright alright . . . Well I have an idea. We form a team. 3 of us. We plan and work. We try our level best to get the best we can. But we won't put everything on the line and work in a normal way that we do. But this time together as a team and a bit more low profile. That way we would be safe and also we would be able to make some change, if not much . . . . How's that???"

"Well I think that's fantastic. I am in." Prithvi chimed in.

"I think that's a fair point." Anjali agreed rubbing her hand on her husband's shoulder.

"Well if this is what you all want then I guess I don't have another option, do I??" Adhiraj replied with the hint from Anjali and a submission in his voice. "I'm in too . . . ."

"That's like my son . . ." Daksh teased him and punched him lightly on his shoulder. Everybody laughed.

"*Chal* . . . it's getting late now . . . . *Mujhe kal subah office bhi jana hai* . . ." Adhiraj said getting up.

When they started walking back to their respective cars . . . Prithvi suddenly asked Adhiraj finding him alone for a minute. "Dude what's the matter? You seem kind of you know . . . upset . . . As a matter of fact I have been noticing the moment we met. Is there something troubling you?"

"Well you know it's just the pressure of work. I will be honest with you guys. It's just that the current political situation is unstable and unsafe for everybody. I just want you guys and your families safe." Adhiraj replied." And well Anjana Roy is doing or rather trying to do the same job. But you see even she isn't succeeding."

"Hmmmm . . . I get it . . . So you mean that the sort of efforts she is putting in is not enough. Well we will have to do something. We all meet at Daksh's place on Friday in the evening. We make a good working plan. In the meanwhile I want you to organize as much as information as you can about the different major pillars in politics." said Prithvi.

"Well it's all settled then. See you guys on Friday." Prithvi said as he and Avni got in to the jeep and said a goodbye followed by Adhiraj's Mercedes.

On the way home, as Adhiraj was driving, Anjali put her hand on his shoulder and said, "You really lost you cool today? That was actually a rare sight."

Adhiraj smiled in return "I didn't really . . . I had to fake it . . . they are adamant on joining politics. And given the current situation . . . I am looking forward to cut all ties . . . not making new ones or reviving old ones . . ."

"Hmmm . . . . You know your friend earns almost 100 times a normal journalist."

"You felt so too?" Adhiraj looked at her.

"Hahaha you know once she took me to the bedroom to show her shopping . . . Trust me that girl has got some real expensive taste. And given the size of her wardrobe, she is either a very good shoplifter or her husband works for some secret spy agency that pays him a fortune."

"Hahaha . . . well for the record, Charvi's father is very rich. So that is also one possible explanation."

"Hmmmm . . . . By the way, you know you can't possibly expose ALL the corrupt politicians. That is impossible for you. You know what I mean. This team and stuff. Where are you going with this Adhir?" Anjali continued.

Adhiraj looked at her and in the most innocent voice he could pull up, "I don't know what you are talking about." Anjali laughed.

"By the way . . . what was that shoulder rub for?" Adhiraj continued.

"Common . . . you know what that was about."

"I am really a bad influence on you." Adhiraj laughed.

"Oh no . . . I was always like this . . . You know when I was young, I used to think that given my tastes and preferences . . . My marital life would be extremely boring . . . especially when I was to become a housewife. But well thanks to you . . . . I get to enjoy a little."

"Hahaha . . . . Same here . . . . And are you really 27?" Adhiraj looked at her.

"Well I prefer 24 but yeah . . . why?"

"Wow . . . I thought you were around 25 . . ."

"Well does it make any difference?" she came closer.

""Of course it makes a lot of difference. You still aren't a mother." Adhiraj looked back and forth between her and the road.

"Well for that, you will have to work lesser in the office and harder in the bed." She almost whispered in his ear, biting his earlobe.

"Hahaha let me drive . . . we are almost home."

. . . .

CHAPTER 4

A couple of days later, Daksh's office.

DAKSH WAS AS USUAL SITTING in his office, which was like any other modern day offices, nothing out of the usual, a personal computer on the left side of his table, a laptop in front and a couple of files sprawled on the empty space. Both the screens were on, but he was lost somewhere, pondering over the day's events when suddenly his phone rang. It was his friend from Bhopal, Anil Kumar, who was a like-minded guy and on many occasions had worked with Daksh to uncover small scandals and sting operations.

"Hi brother . . . how are you?" A hearty smile came on Daksh's face.

"I am good. What happened to you? I heard you quit the job and shifted to Delhi 2 days ago." Anil blurted out all at once.

"Well the circumstances changed . . . I got a really good job offer and since it was in Delhi, it was too good to pass up. In fact, today was my first day here. Its too good man . . . something like a dream come true for people like us."

"Still . . . you could have informed me . . . I went out of station to cover a story and when I came back today, I found out that you have shifted."

"Yeah . . . didn't have time . . . you know such jobs don't wait for too long . . ."

"Oh . . . for a moment I thought that it was because of the mess that happened with the minister . . . anyways it's good to hear that you got a better job in a better place . . . see if there is a vacancy for me . . . even I am starting to get bored with the narrow scope of politics in this state."

"Well, trust me with two things . . . no politics has a narrow scope for too long, and second the further you are from politics the more are you safe and happy."

"Yeah I know . . . but that's the fun isn't it . . ." Daksh knew that Anil was smiling from ear to ear.

"By the way," Anil continued, "do you know that Anjana's movement have gone down in Madhya Pradesh? People are losing interest and today on the fifth day of her strike the number of people almost went half of what it was on the first day. If this continued she is doomed to fail soon."

"Yes I am aware. Her methods are old and time consuming. People in today's world neither have the time nor the energy to quit their work and continue in an eternal conflict." Daksh replied.

"What you are saying is true. And that's why I think somebody will have to back her up. I mean she needs some seriously strong support else the movement will come down within a month."

"Let's see if we could do something. I mean we are at the same level now and if she really wants the same thing as we do, we will definitely support her." Daksh continued.

Soon Anil bid his goodbye and best wishes to Daksh and promised to keep him informed about the major activities on the state level.

As Anil hung up, Daksh realized that what Adhiraj said had turned out to be true after all. The government's plan was working. Their patience was wearing Anjana Roy's movement out. She was losing support. If this goes on for the next few weeks, she will have to call off her movement. He turned on the TV to watch the latest updates. It was the breaking news everywhere. After all the promises that Anjana had made, she failed to gain public support and so she was forced to review her plans about the movement and had to postpone it to the later part of the next month. This wasn't a good news for anybody who wanted a corruption free India. He checked his watch. It was almost 8. 'Time to go home,' he thought. He called in his secretary, Neena. And there walked in the 25 year old goddess in her cat walk fashion that drove men crazy. He gave her an uncomfortable smile and she replied in her typical confident and yet polite smile. He asked for his schedule the next day and made small plans.

Soon he was in his car driving back home . . . "I don't have any idea what you are talking about." He retorted in anger. "Well you better get an understanding of the situation Daksh, because if you don't, then there will be actions whose consequences we both will regret." . . . He remembered the conversation like it happened a minute ago. It still rang in his ears. The traffic in this area was not much. It was a good locality, calm and peaceful. This all should be over soon. He saw the photo of his lovely wife on the deck smiling back at him. Thousands of thoughts came in his mind . . . most of them were anger and remorse . . . he looked at the photo again and pushed the thoughts away . . . 'This should have turned out better.' He thought to himself as he continued to drive.

. . . .

February 2012, Daksh's house.

Prithvi rang the doorbell outside Daksh's medium and yet lavish house. Such a house in this area was quite an achievement. With a small but tended garden outside, with beautiful arrays of flowers, few of which he recognized to be champa, lilies and roses . . . 'Maybe in another life . . .' he thought to himself. Soon Charvi opened the door and called him. He said hi to her and came in to find Daksh and Adhiraj sitting on the sofa laughing and having snacks. This was the trademark of their friendship ever since. No matter how serious the situation was, Daksh always lured the other two into candid talks and snacks. Childhood memories refreshed, Prithvi smiled and joined them.

"Hey do you remember sandy?" Daksh asked Prithvi as soon as he sat down,

"Sandy?"

"Yeah, the girl who lived down the road. I heard she had a huge crush on you. And even after knowing this, you didn't even try to make a move on her." Daksh said as he and Adhiraj burst out laughing and Prithvi got a bit uncomfortable.

"Look . . . Prithvi still regrets it." Adhiraj nudged him.

"Hey . . . guys common . . . offer variation to convention. We have been doing this all our lives. I think we should get serious now." Prithvi tried his bid.

"Ok ok . . . . Lets get serious . . . BTW, when I went back home last summer, I heard she got married to a policeman in our locality." Daksh looked at him. "So she was into policemen?" Adhiraj looked at Daksh all innocent.

"Apparently, the guy she was into, turned out to be the policeman." Daksh grinned.

"So does Avni know about Sandy?" Adhiraj winked at Prithvi.

"Hahaha . . . . Well if she doesn't . . . we will tell her."

"Yeah, well, CHARVI . . . can you come here for a minute? I need to tell you something about Daksh's youth adventures." Prithvi called out.

"Dude . . . you can't break our promise. Not a word about the past to any wife whatsoever."

'Well I guess I can."

"No no . . . Adhir . . . Start the meeting . . . tell us the basics." Daksh literally pleaded. He knew if the secrets opened, he would be the one who will get into most trouble. But somewhere in the back of his head . . . he knew Prithvi would never do such a thing.

"Hahaha . . . ok . . . everybody ready?." Adhiraj asked.

"Well go ahead." Daksh assured.

"I'll tell you about the big fishes first." And so Adhiraj started.

. . . .

"First, Rajaswamy Mohan, the most well-known face in the Indian politics. The backbone of Bharat Jan-hit party. According to most of the people, he is one of the most passive gamers of politics. But only an inside guy like me knows that he is the actual leader of the party. Only the party people know and value his importance. He is like the uncrowned king of the party. Whenever anything wrong happens, Mohan gets them out. The smartest of all and the most important of all. If you are able to get him, then you have half of your politics conquered."

"So you mean to say he is like a consultant. A contingency. The strongest card. If we get him out of the game, your party, Jan-hit party won't survive?" Daksh got interested.

"Well the party won't be uprooted, but yeah it would be like removing 2 out of 4 legs of a chair. And same can be said about his son, Ranvijay, who is about to join in the next couple of years and unlike his father, he will be aiming the throne . . ."

"Well let's not talk about the to-be corrupts . . . let's talk about the present." Jai interfered.

"Ok . . . Next, number second, Rahman Malik, Rajaswamy's right hand. He is the very reason why nobody ever finds about the black money and all those scams involving crores and crores of rupees. Every time something comes up, he gets the money accounts manipulated and all that remains is shit. He works mostly on Rajaswamy's signals but sometimes he works on his own, and for his own."

"Hmm . . . so when we take him out . . . your party goes bankrupt." Jai sighed.

"Yes . . . you take him out . . . and Jan-hit party will lose hold of most of the major scams and frauds."

"Anybody else?" Daksh started getting a little impatient.

"Number 3 on this list is Rajeev Sinha, another mastermind, the current chief minister, who keeps an eye on the vote bank of the party and devises new ways of pulling down the opposition parties . . . . like the current opposition, Alliance party. He is also known to be having some underworld connections recently."

"And finally the number 4, the opposition leader, Ramakant Yadav, who is well, Alliance's version of Rajaswamy. Probably the most active member of today's politics. Very intelligent, very clever, very smart."

"I don't know much about opposition, just almost the same amount of knowledge as you. We don't have any inside people in their party that I know of."

"Hmmm . . . never mind . . . we could always start from your party . . . And continue this across the country." Jai grinned.

"Hahaha . . . So this is the 90% of the politics in front of you. These guys have a major hand in running politics. If you get even any 2 or 3 of these, you have done a very good job for the country. Rest all are pawns. You won't gain much by screwing them," Adhiraj sighed as he finished and rolled back in the sofa . . . taking a deep breath.

"So this was what you had to give us. I mean we should know what is happening and why is it happening . . . there's another name in the headlines these days . . . Anjana Roy . . . who is she??? I think we should keep her in the agenda too . . . Where did she come from and what is her motive. It would be foolishness to trust her completely. So tell us about her as well. I mean the inside information that media does not tell the public." Daksh said.

Adhiraj took a deep breath. Daksh noticed that he didn't seem too comfortable.

"Ok if that's what you want to know," Adhiraj continued, "Anjana Roy, as you know is a social activist. Presenting a very ideal image of herself and a concern for the country and countrymen, she has gained huge public support. However, after digging a lot, contradicting to her common man image, it has been found that she owns lots of money. But on papers she does not have anything more than ordinary. Following the paper trails and investigating, we have found that all her money and investment is in the form of a charitable trust, Shantiniketan, which is known to fund all the different activities of Anjana and her coworkers. We have sources that tell us that Shantiniketan is actually funded by Anjana Roy herself. She distributes her black money among her foreign contacts and her big supporters in India. She gives them money under the table, which they very smoothly donate her back through the trust. We tried to trace the contacts but all the transactions in the trust are anonymous and the connections of Anjana Roy are all indirect. This is making it real hard to prove this theory. Rajaswamy has kept his best men after Anjana Roy all the time, and this is the latest information that we have right now. But I am sure that there is a lot more, which may never be revealed. But yes, one developing theory is that Anjana Roy has some personal motive behind this movement. The reason is that in the 52 years of her life she does not have any record of any social work. In fact, you will be surprised to know that Anjana Roy was born probably 4 years ago. The trust has been setup just 3 years ago and it has been funded heavily since then, a lot more than any other trust. So it's pretty clear that it's pretty well planned." Adhiraj stated.

"Wait a minute. What do you mean by she was born probably 4 years ago." Daksh interrupted.

"Well we were trying to track her past down . . . you know anything we can get our hands on . . . a weak spot . . . anything that will keep her quiet. But her life before 2008 does not have any record. So it can mean either of the two things . . . She has had some real connections who wiped her information out of every major database, or second, she is somebody else. I mean she is using an alias. She is someone else in real life."

"But what about the things that she was saying on the media when questioned about her background. What was that all about???" Jai broke his silence for the first time.

"Well she claims that she her only motive is to see a corruption free India, and her family is the whole country. And also that her struggle has nothing to do with her personal life, present or past."

"Hahaha . . . . Well jokes apart, I think that's enough for today, now I think we should know a bit more about Anjana Roy, I don't know why but I have a feeling that she has some deep connection with someone we might be interested in."

"Actually you are right . . . there are rumors that she has terrorist connections and she is being funded from Pakistan." Adhiraj continued. "If any of that is true, then we might be on something big here."

"But don't you think that we should target the politicians first, who are actually corrupt." Daksh broke in.

"Well why do you want to do that? I mean we cannot target my party at the start because if it goes down, I, if not much, will lose my power and credibility. And the opposition, well it is also a rumor that Anjana has connections with the opposition. They planted her to show BJHP down, so that Alliance could take control. And suppose, if this isn't all true, and she actually is trying to do something for the country, we can always help her with the cause."

"Hmmm, maybe you are right . . . anyways . . . lets at least start, we will see where this road takes us." Daksh retracted.

"So Adhiraj I want you to find out as much as you can in your office, Jai in the police records, and I will look for her in the old journals and articles. I think that would be a good way to start. Let's find out about her as much as we can before we plan our plan of action."

"Yup . . . and we get in touch as soon as someone finds out anything."

. . . .

CHAPTER 5

A few days later, India news agency HQ

HE LOOKED OUT OF THE window of his office on the 12th floor as several thoughts raced in his mind. The otherwise beautiful office filled with an air of fun and candidness was filled with sullenness and tension. It had been 3 weeks since he had started looking up for Anjana Roy. But he hadn't found even a single trace. For the first time in his life, he felt desperation crawling up in his head. He knew the stakes, and they were very high. He was running out of time. When he started failing up with the facts, he tried to come up with some logical explanation but couldn't succeed their either. 'What can be the reason???Why is she doing it??? There's no trace of any social activity or public help in the past. Adhiraj was right, it is as if Anjana Roy was born just 5 years ago. No records. Even if she lived her life as a common woman, there must be something.' Daksh kept thinking to himself. His patience was wearing out. He was giving his best but couldn't find anything about her past. He looked back at the table to find his secretary, Neena working in a seat opposite to his chair, busy in her laptop . . . he looked at her uncomfortably then returned his absent-minded gaze back to the streets. He decided to call Adhiraj to see if he got his hands on anything. But he was disappointed there as well. He continued gazing at the busy streets as hundreds of cars passed him. He knew the time was very less. Anjana Roy had to be brought down one way or the other. And it had to be done fast. He looked back at his 22 year old sizzling secretary in her formal executive suit that ran down to just above her knees, her milky white legs one over the other, a white blouse that did so little to conceal the beauty that lay within, going up and down with every breath, his thoughts took a turn and he looked down on the ground. Then as he looked back at her face, she was looking at him smiling in that innocuous manner, her eyes like that of a child's . . .

"What happened sir?"

He smiled and nodded and said,

"You know you are too hot for a secretary."

"Hahaha . . . sir, stop it. You know I wanted to be a great journalist. Just like you are. Letting the people know the true image of their country. Journalism is one of the greatest jobs a person can do for their country."

"Yeah it's true. We do a great work. Sometimes when we expose someone, or help out people through media, even I feel very happy within."

"Yes . . . but unfortunately I couldn't get a good college, so I here I am . . . hoping to become a journalist someday . . . but its still great working for you, you know. Everybody knows the kind of scams and people you have exposed in the past."

"Hahaha . . . I wished for that . . . and I did that . . . and then I realised the true meaning of the saying . . . be careful for what you wish for, cuz you just might get it."

"I didn't get you sir. You should be happy instead of being so thoughtful . . ."

"I'll tell you some other day . . . when the time is right . . ." He said as he took out a cigarette from his shirt pocket and lit it . . . took a deep drag and sighed in anticipation of the events to come.

. . . .

It was 3 weeks since they started digging about Anjana Roy. The goal was clear, if her intentions were good get along with her, else destroy her to the core. But this wasn't producing results. She was creating a complete havoc in the country, and off late had raised a demand for re-elections which had set the BJHP all aggravated. To top it off, some of the prominent ministers declared their support for her anti corruption movement in the country on national media and also made a promise that they would help her if needed. This empowerment was all that was needed to fuel her movement. Time was slipping like sand in a fist. They all decided to meet and if nothing else, change their strategy. Their hard work hadn't bore any fruits. So on the very same day, they all gathered at Daksh's place again, to discuss their leads. "How is this possible, it's as if she appeared out of nowhere. I have checked all the news records for anything about her. Abhi checked in on the police records and the criminal records but we couldn't find a trace of her existence. This is a fake identity. I am sure it is." Daksh let out all at once. Adhiraj noticed that out of the three he was the most desperate. Being a member of BJHP, he was really worried but Daksh seemed to be in a bad situation. But then it could be just the pressure of his work mounting. Thinking thus he ignored him and spoke "well I have a small lead. Now I don't know if its big but we might be onto something here."

"What is it?" Daksh's eyes lightened up.

"I was just going through the speeches of Anjana Roy and I noticed a pattern in her accusations."

"What do you mean?"

"Well her accusations are very specific. I know we have discussed this before that she has some internal contacts. What I am trying to say is, she is targeting a very specific section of people."

"Nope I still don't get you. Elaborate."

"Well she keeps on talking about removing corruption, but over the last year, she is accusing most of the politicians of BJHP and only a handful of Alliance and practically not even a single politician in other party."

"So???"

"So, it is a very good chance that she is a pawn of someone in Alliance."

"But if this is the case, why would she blame even a single member of Alliance."

"Maybe because Alliance wants to remove the dirt from their party. You know, internal politics in a party."

"Well you are right. We are onto something here. If we could just find out the common enemy of all the politicians accused, we will have the person who holds the leash on Anjana Roy." Daksh sounded finally excited.

"Well why don't we go and meet her, have a talk with her, but on a different note. Daksh, you go, we try to arrange a personal meet between you two and if we succeed in getting her talking and she might spill something, who knows where we get."

"Well but I want to ask something." Abhi broke his silence for the first time in the evening. "Why are we targeting Anjana Roy if there is not a proper lead on her? I know that we doubt her. But we DOUBT her.

There are many other people whom we can target. Like the ones in BJHP we were talking the other day."

"Well for starters, she has a fake identity. And don't you think that somebody would decide to give up everything for a pure selfless reason. There are people who love doing things for their country, but this is too much. And we cannot start with my party directly because the moment I stand up against my party, I'll lose all the power and my life would be in grave danger."

"There can be some people willing to give up everything for their country. And besides it is very probable that she changed her identity to protect her loved ones. She knew that once she opens fire against the politicians everybody will be after her. Journalists, politicians, police . . . practically everybody who is related to the corrupt politicians and could get hurt with their decline." Prithvi argued.

"What you are saying is probable but what about the accusations on her. I told you she was accused of connections with underworld, her funding from the black money and so on . . . the list is endless . . . they must be at least based on something . . . . The smoke might not be caused by the forest fire but at least there is always a flame, no matter how small, at the heart of smoke. She can be doing something selflessly for the country but at the same time this is also very much probable that she has some selfish motives."

"Hmmm well in that case we should get our doubts cleared. I think you should go ahead with the plan." Prithvi sighed.

"Alright then, I will try to set up an interview with her as quickly as I can. In the meanwhile, I think you two should follow the lead Adhiraj has so brilliantly managed to spot." Daksh said.

"Hahaha . . . It's settled then. But it's getting a bit late. I think I'll take leave. See you guys." Saying Adhiraj departed with a broad smile on his face.

. . . .

Next morning, Adhiraj's mansion.

"Hey bhagwan . . . mujhe aapne sab kuch diya. Bas isi tarah apni nazar mujhpar banaye rakhna. Mujhe aap pr poora bharosa hai ki mujhe jab jis cheez ki zarurat hogi, aap bina maange hi de denge . . ."

Adhiraj got down on his knees and touched his forehead on the ground in front of the large idol of Hanuman Ji in his own small but very lavish temple built on the first floor of his house. His devotion towards his God was remarkable. He liked to keep it a secret for some reason.

"I still sometimes don't understand the way you work things." His wife smiled as he came down on the ground floor and sat for breakfast with his wife.

"What?"

"The conversation you had last night with your friends. I thought they were your true friends."

"Yes they are . . . They mean a lot to me."

"Do you think what you are doing is right?"

"Well I don't know. I seriously don't know. All I know right now is that I dreamt something when I was a kid. The dream became my life. And now when I have got this close, I don't want to give it away."

"You know a person should be very careful of what he wishes . . . because our dreams define us. They shape our very existence. They become who we are. So we should choose very wisely. And right now, for some reason, I think you should think of some other plan. This con might not give you the happiness you deserve."

"Hmmm I understand what you are saying. But it's done now. It cannot be taken back. I am in this 100%. And I want you. Without you I my dream would never become a reality."

"Hey . . . I am with you till death . . . no matter what happens. I would leave my entire world to live a day of our lives together happily."

"Well then I don't want anything else. I trust you." So saying he kissed his wife's hand.

. . . .

A few days later . . .

"Sir, just one interview, it could change lives of millions of people . . . yes sir, I understand, at most it would take one hour . . . and besides it would help Miss Anjana to spread her message more clearly . . . thank you sir . . . thank you . . . . I'll be really grateful to you for this favor." saying so Daksh hung up. He got his interview with Anjana Roy, finally . . . it hadn't been easy though . . . he had to use all his contacts to get an interview with Anjana Roy in a one to one situation . . . no interference and no objections . . . 'this is it . . . 'he thought . . .' I have my chance to see the woman who shook the lives of so many including him . . . if only I could eliminate her . . . things might go back to the normal.'

He started his preparations straight away, making phone calls, organizing his questions, doing his homework . . . this was something that had always wanted to do . . . make smart and confident people sweat . . . it was his job . . . and he loved it . . . he always did . . . but now this was bigger than anything he had ever done . . . this was personal . . . Maybe Adhiraj was right . . . she has been planted by politicians . . . but which ones? Adhiraj's theory seemed true but it actually did contradict the whole truth itself. Anyways . . . that's another day's food for thought. First things first. The interview with Anjana Roy was all that he could think of. And thinking thus he dozed off.

. . . .

Anjana Roy's house.

Daksh was dumbstruck with the beauty and grace he witnessed. Anjana Roy was finally standing in front of him and this was the first time that he was seeing her in real life. A very wise face on a body covered with white saree that had red borders. And a very beautiful shawl draped over her shoulders. Even at her age she seemed beautiful. And despite all her authority and status, there she was standing with a very comforting smile and a motherly look in her eyes.

"Namaste Ms. Anjana Roy, sorry, Ms. or Mrs.???" Started Daksh with his typical smile.

"You can call me whatever you like, but I really prefer Miss." Anjana smiled and replied. "I really like to get things straight Mr. Daksh. So tell me, why did you want to have a very private interview with me? It's coming in the news tomorrow, isn't it?"

"Well of course not all of it. See I like to get to the point rather beating around the bush . . . To be honest, I like meeting smart people . . . people of your cadre."

"And by my cadre you mean?"

"The big fishes in politics."

"Hahaha okay. So ask whatever's on your mind."

"Well one simple question, why do you hate politics so much. From the day you have become the celebrity in the news channels you have just gone on and on about the flaws in our system and the corruption."

"Well, do you love politics??" Anjana coolly smiled. "I don't think any true Indian does, especially after the secrets that we came to know recently . . . . Am I right???"

"Yes you are absolutely right. But one thing that really amazes me is the thing which nobody thought of doing before and nobody could do before, you were able to accomplish it really easily??What's the reason behind this grand success???"

"We haven't got the success yet son . . . . we are still a long way . . . . It's just the first step that's successful . . ."

"Then what will be success for you Ma'am???"

"A corruption free, completely educated and a world leader India will be success for us."

"That's a really good thought. But politicians say that most of your supporter have been bought. You are paying them to be with you. What have you got in reply for that?"

"We had the proofs of corruption, we just showed it to the people and got them aware, and that's all. This was the reason of our public support. Every true Indian is supporting us and will support us."

"But don't you think that it is strange that the secrets that were guarded by some of the highest minds in the country were revealed by a simple woman?"

"Well this is politics my dear. Someday someone had to. And why??? You think woman cannot be smart??? You see, every person who commits a sin makes a mistake . . . leaves a trail behind him. Me and a couple of my supporters just followed those trails, and got our hands on a few evidences. And that's where we started, and since then we have never looked back. And those supporters prefer to stay in the darkness so I came into the light. How long I have to live, say 20 more years, I don't have anybody in this world to call my own except my country. India is my home and Indians are my family. I just am working to give my family a better life."

"Yes definitely Ma'am, you have really great thoughts. I don't say this very often but your love for your country touched my heart. If you need any help of any sort . . . you can always rely on me. By the way a couple of more question mam, if you don't mind???"

"Thank you son . . . Yes go on . . ."

"Ma'am people have been looking for you for a while now, but nobody found any records about your past life. Much less anything about any political activity or social work, what suddenly prompted a feeling of such a great love for your country and fueled it enough to start a national movement????"

"Well as I told you that I don't have anybody in this world to call my own except my country, that's why I decided to do this job, and it's not sudden. Not at all . . . it was always there . . . and I always preferred to do my works anonymously because I don't like to take credit for doing something good for the people of our country. And the planning for this movement started years back. The preparations took so long. And to be honest with you, I was really reluctant to come into light, but this movement wasn't possible if I stayed in darkness. So here I am . . ."

"That's really nice to hear ma'am. Did you have any source of inspiration???"

"Mahatma Gandhi, baapu, the great man who inspired me since childhood, when I read about him in the school, and ever since then I have lived my life for my country."

"Great ma'am, you are really inspiring me to come and join you in this second struggle for real independence . . . ."

"Hahaha . . . it would be great if you would come . . . trust me . . . doing something with a pure selfless heart has its own happiness, fulfilling true happiness." So saying she smirked at him

"Hahaha . . . I know ma'am . . . I have experienced it myself . . . just one more question . . . the last one I promise . . . what about your past . . . you must be having a real family at some point in time . . . parents, siblings, a husband children . . . what happened to them???"

She kept her calm but Daksh could swear he saw a hint of emotion for the first time for just a couple of moments in her eyes

"My family died a few years ago and that was a totally different life. I was a housewife then . . . . other than this I don't have any past." So saying she smiled contentedly at him

He got up signaling with his body language that the interview was over and the smile on his face meant he was satisfied, "Thank you mam, if you need any sort of help, please let me know, I am always ready for it. Thanks for giving me your invaluable time, I'll be greatful to you. Thank you mam."

She smiled in reply as he exited her office. She took a moment to compose herself. She took out a photo of a beautiful young girl from her purse and looked at it longingly as a tear droplet fell from her eye onto the old photo.

. . . .

CHAPTER 6

Next morning, India news HQ.

"How was the interview sir?" Neena chirped as soon as Daksh entered his cabin the next morning. 'God I love this girl.' He thought to himself and smiled.

"It was fantastic . . ." he replied as he took in the very familiar lovely scent of his cabin . . . it was that particular fresh morning where the sun shines bright and soothing making you feel good, and putting a genuine smile on your face . . . the scent of the room was partially due to the freshness and partially because of Neena's strong perfume. "Any phone calls or something???" He said as he took his chair and signaled her to sit in the opposite one. Though his life was full of worries, besides her wife, only this girl had that amazing smile which touched his heart at the bottom.

"No sir."

"Okay . . . umm . . . why don't you go and get two cups of coffee??? Let's have today's coffee together."

"Yeah sure sir" she smiled and got up keeping the papers and files on the table.

"Thanks sweetheart . . ." he replied with a smile and watched her go. Damn this girl. The interview of the day before had put him in a total fix. There were three faces in the situation. One was Adhiraj's view, the one he believed was true, second Anjana's view which he wished was wrong and third his view which was a pure act of desperation. And he had to make a choice. A choice that would define his very existence from that day onwards. He had lived his life like the waves in an ocean . . . never caring about what others wished or wanted . . . a free willed and yet very determined life . . . that was till 2 months ago where he finally crashed into a mountain. And he decided to bend his way and move according to the rock rather than trying to fight and die out. And that choice had left him feeling all guilty and remorseful. Everyday had become a burden on him. In the meanwhile he took up smoking to relax his nerves but to no avail. And even after all that remorse and guilt he was still very much relentless to get back to his old lifestyle. But there didn't seem a way out. He had to bend himself or else he could get cut. Maybe in the long run he might be able to figure a way out. But right now . . . desperation and remorse seemed to be the way of life . . .

"Sir . . . here is our coffee . . . with two cubes of sugar as you like." Neena came in with a tray in her hand and a smile on her blood red lips.

"Thank you Neena."

"Sir I think you should not smoke in the morning."

That was when he realized he had lit a cigarette involuntarily and had taken almost 8 drags.

. . . .

Adhiraj's mansion, later that afternoon.

"Dada I am really confused." Adhiraj said in a worried tone.

"What's the matter son?"

"Dada I value my dreams a lot. But not this way. This might not turn out well."

"Son you have to understand one thing . . . everything in this world comes with a price. And a man is nothing but his choices. You have to understand these two things."

"I know dada. Every time I had things my way. I bent people and situations to fit my way and give me the kind of return I wanted. But this time I am unsure about the results."

"Son, you are extremely smart and careful. Trust yourself. You have all what it takes to make this con successful. A few months ago when you told me what exactly you wanted out of politics, the only reason I stopped you was because of the instability and lack of the money. Given the circumstances you know we could not afford to give you what you wanted. And then we devised this plan to give you the kind of life you wanted . . . something that would benefit both of us tremendously. Don't forget your goals son. Don't forget why you started. You know your purpose in life. It's very good. Now you have to work for it. Don't worry about your future. Everything you want in your future is lying in a vault waiting to be grabbed by you. Stay focused. Alright?"

"Ji dada. I will. Whatever happens, I won't back down from here."

"It will be good son. Trust me. It will be good."

. . . .

Daksh's house, Saturday evening.

"I would like this one." So saying Adhiraj picked up the sweet and salty snack from the cupboard in the kitchen.

"Knock yourself out." Replied Charvi smiling. "Hey, by the way, did you see the new TV we bought yesterday?"

"No. Daksh didn't mention it."

"Oh come with me. It's installed in our bedroom. And call Prithvi also. It's one of those LED kinds . . . 40" . . . really expensive." Charvi grinned from ear to ear with proud.

Prithvi and Daksh joined Adhiraj who was following a very chirpy and excited Charvi who was walking very fast to her bedroom.

"Here it is. Isn't it great?" She said pointing to sleek black LED TV installed in front of the bed, shining brightly under the beautiful yellow lights.

"Wow . . . this is awesome." Adhiraj exclaimed.

"Congrats man." Prithvi shook hands with Daksh.

"Thanks bro." Daksh smiled uncomfortably.

Prithvi was last in the awe of the room. The dim yellow lights that added to the aura of the room were doing a perfect job. A large painting of horses running in a field on a rainy day was covering the wall on the left side. There were fresh flowers on the bedside table. The wall on the right side was three deeply set cupboards and a door that was a washroom. Overall the room was a little bigger than medium but extremely rich in the feel. The walls were painted with a rich color and the bed was a king sized extravagant bed with probably silken sheets by the look of it.

Adhiraj wasn't much affected by the aura of the room. Though there was something that caught his eye. There were about 10 Louis Vuitton and Armani shopping bags stuffed in the dustbin by the bed and by the size of it the dust bin must have been cleared in the very morning. Daksh and Charvi did dress well but he never suspected them to be this. Anjali was right then. He was secretly very rich and his wife's expensive tastes were giving him away. He made it a mental note to find out about his past. His actions in the last 10 years might give him an insight as to what had made him that he was today. Given his job he couldn't afford half of what he was comfortably spending. And still after all this kind of money, Daksh didn't seem too happy. The very confident and no-care-for-anybody guy seemed thoughtful. 12 years cannot change that much in a man.

"I think we should go down." Daksh's voice broke his thoughts.

"Dude what are you thinking about?" Daksh looked at him.

"Nothing . . . umm just some things in my office . . . never mind . . . Nice room by the way."

"Thank you. This is all her doing." Hearing this Charvi blushed.

. . . .

"So any developments?" Daksh started as the 3 friends finally sat on the sofa in the living room.

"Nothing from my side." Prithvi declared.

"Same here." Adhiraj said.

"I too have got nothing." Daksh replied.

There was an awkward silence in the room for a couple of minutes which was broken by Prithvi.

"I don't understand why we are trying to swim in the shallow water. Why don't we pick up any other lead? Why are we constantly trying to prove Anjana Roy guilty?"

"We are not trying to prove Anjana Roy guilty Prithvi. According to Adhiraj, she has definitely some connections with the Alliance and he has a very sordid reason for that belief. So Anjana Roy is just the start. We had to start from somewhere. And I am totally convinced that chasing Anjana Roy won't go in vain."

"Hey wait wait wait . . . what if she has only one connection?" Adhiraj broke in.

"What do you mean?" Prithvi looked at him.

"Yes this is it. The only reason why there is not much about her is because she has only one contact."

"I still don't understand what you are saying."

"I'll tell you a very short story. Once there was a guy. He was rejected and neglected by even his own family. Somehow, he met a man who was at the very top of the world. Now this man saw a great potential in this young guy and decided to give him a chance to prove his smartness. But the young guy wanted something different from life. He had his own dreams. And because this man was at the very top, it wasn't hard for him to fulfill this young guy's dreams. The man was in a very big trouble. His throne was in danger. So they made a promise to each other. This young guy would learn the rules of the game under this man and help him out of his troubles and return his throne to him in return for his dreams. The young guy reached the very top without any connections or proper education . . . In fact he made his way so quickly up to the top that except the man who taught him, nobody got the time to study him and find out what or who he was before this."

"Okay okay okay . . . . I see the point you are trying to make here."

"Yes . . . so the two morals of this story is?" Adhiraj continued.

"First, if someone is doing something, it doesn't mean that they are interested in the outcome of the journey. The result can be just a part of the bargain that is made with someone who is not anywhere near the picture.

And second, if you sneak your way up with a very specific line of thought and action, you don't attract much attention." Daksh finished Adhiraj's sentence.

"Exactly." Adhiraj grinned.

"By the way, who is the guy and the man in the story?"

"The story is true of course, but nobody knows the two characters. I just happened to be a listener when this story was being told in a group of people."

"Well so how do we proceed with Anjana Roy? Though the story has given us some clue, we are still at the exact same point where we started."

"No we aren't. Look at it this way. If she is an ally of the alliance, then that special contact must be a member of the alliance. We just have to find out who?" Adhiraj got excited.

Hearing this Daksh's eyes lit up. The picture all of a sudden seemed to be very clear. 'This is all Alliance's game. The whole country is suffering from their internal party politics.'

"So," Adhiraj continued, "Now we know where to look. Get all your sources at work. Daksh and Prithvi, talk to all your informers and contacts. I want each and every detail on each member of Alliance. In the meanwhile, there is a matter that requires my attention. I'll look into that and get back to you as soon as possible."

"Alright. But you know Adhiraj time is life at this moment. We need to work fast and efficiently. We don't have much time." Daksh said.

"Yes I know. Trust me the work I am talking about is also a matter of life and death if not sorted out in time. And yes one more thing, do your work as silently as you can. Now that you are so close to politics, don't trust anybody. Be very careful and smart, because one wrong move and boom . . . before you realize, your whole world will be turned upside down. Every step with caution and thought."

'I know buddy I know . . . the price of wrong move really turns your world upside down . . .' thinking thus Daksh sighed.

. . . .

CHAPTER 7

Next morning, Adhiraj's mansion.

"Dada I need to find out about Daksh Singhvi in Bhopal. Get our best people to look into it. My instincts tell me that he is suspicious."

"Why? I thought he was your friend."

"Yes he is supposed to be. But he is also supposed to be a middle class honest but smart guy who should have seen through the game."

"Maybe he trusts you."

"Dada, as far as I know Daksh, he is too smart to believe or trust anybody. He won't do a single thing that would be selfless. And above all, the truth is . . . I somehow don't trust him. There are a lot of things he is hiding. Let's get his intel and we will know if my doubts have any existence in reality."

"Okay, I trust your instinct. I'll contact Bhopal tomorrow itself and do the needful. Message me his picture and other details. I'll get the intel ASAP."

"Thank you dada." So saying Adhiraj hung up and relaxed on his bed.

'Daksh is a smart guy. And the smarter the guy is, the harder it is to contain him. And there is something that I am missing. Something that I am seeing and yet not able to process. And till the time I don't know him in and out, it would be a foolishness to trust him. You can never completely trust an extremely smart guy.' Adhiraj was lost in his thoughts when his wife came in with a glass of water. She had seen the gleam of happiness in his eyes after a long time. There were not enough reasons for her husband to be happy but these days after meeting his friends, he had started getting back to his usual mood, a cheerful one, the one filled with hope. She knew how much this meant to him. Both the husband and wife were a happy couple. They snuggled under the blanket. They used to chat and muse over the day's events. They loved each other very much, a rare successful arrange marriage in today's world, a perfect match for each other. Each of them found the other one perfect in his or her role. They never found faults with each other. He loved her very much and she had immense trust in him. They were each other's first love and last too . . . It was the kind of relationship where you felt complete in each other's company. A company that was very well defined on both emotional and physical contexts. She was glad to find a man like him and he was glad to find the woman of his dreams. Though they weren't parents after 4 years of marriage, it didn't seem to affect their relationship. It was what everyone in this world wants. Both believed the other was too good for them and it stayed the same in the 5 years of knowing each other and 4 years of marriage. The love was good, the romance was great and the sex was awesome. If there was something like a perfect relationship, they were very close if not there . . . .

. . . .

A week later . . .

'There were so many things that were unsaid but still clearly understood in politics. This was one of those instances.' mused Daksh as he sat on is computer surfing the net. As he was reading, he came across a news article that was about himself. He didn't know any such article had been published. It was dated 6 months back, and it was about the producer who used to talk young models into having relationships with him, making fake promises of success . . . A smile came across his face as he read all the praising and applauding. 'Those were the days . . .' he never thought or cared about anybody. It was just Daksh Singhvi and success for him. And many people misunderstood his craving for success as patriotism. But again, he didn't care. He wanted to see himself on the top. That was all his life was about. And only he knew that he wasn't that much of a true saint either. Journalism had brought him from a middle class boy, whom nobody knew, to a extremely rich guy whom many people feared and respected. And this was the very sole reason he loved journalism. He was also a good painter. A born artist. And if given a choice, in his other life, he would definitely become a painter. His 30 years of life went in making an existence and the near future didn't seem so bright given his circumstances. I just wanted to have a better life . . .

Just one simple mistake and everything is over. His phone's ringtone buzzed him out of his stream of thoughts . . .

"Hey Daksh, Adhiraj here."

"Yes I know. What happened?"

"I am sending a fax in your office. Make sure nobody except you sees it."

"What is it?"

"It's a messenger of success. Call me back after you see it." So saying Adhiraj hung up.

Daksh immediately got up and went into the common room and stood by the machine. Within a couple of minutes a single fax arrived. It was a picture . . . of three people, a man and a woman and a young girl. The picture was old but still clear . . . and Daksh's eyes popped out in amazement as he realized the woman to be none other than Anjana Roy.

. . . .

Same evening, Zarokha restaurant.

"I really am in love with this place." Prithvi said as they placed the three friends placed their order.

"This is awesome. And there *shahi paneer, dal tadka and aloo mutter* is best. It's a pure Indian restaurant at a very reasonable price." Adhiraj smiled.

"Seriously dude, you should have brought us here earlier. It's been 2 months since I have eaten at a good hotel. The place where I went 2 weeks ago was extremely costly and still couldn't deliver the taste." Daksh complained.

"Hahaha . . . worry nothing of that sort will happen here. Anyways, we should get to the point. You two have seen that pic. Now let me elaborate."

"Go ahead."

"I knew I had seen here somewhere before. This pic is 10 years old. The man is Vijaykant Desai, the MLA from Nehru Nagar, a minister of Alliance. The woman in the pic is his wife, Mrs. Leelawati Desai and the girl is Anchal, there 10 years old daughter, who must be around 20 by now. The girl, as you can see is extremely beautiful . . . people say she was one of those girls who matured a lot faster than others, not physically but emotionally . . . Around 8 years ago, she was sent to a boarding school, and these two filed for a divorce. Mrs. Leelawati filed for divorce and accused her husband as a drunkard and corrupt. However the case never really started because Vijaykant literally bought everyone including Leelawati's lawyer. He didn't want a divorce because he thought it would affect his political image. He also paid 5 crores as a gift to her. After that she remained quiet."

"Hmmm . . . it still does not explain the revolution." Daksh said.

"I think it does . . . the politicians whom Anjana Roy has targeted does not include Vijaykant Desai. So it can be that Vijaykant is the mastermind behind this whole game." Adhiraj continued.

"It can be . . . It can very well be . . . This is her one contact . . . somehow the husband and wife have fallen in love again and their love has increased so much that they are shaking the whole country."

"Yeah . . . . So what is the next plan of action?"

"We know there is a fire. We just need to prove it. And once it is proven, Anjana Roy and some ministers of Alliance, both will go down." Adhiraj smiled saying this, but he noticed Daksh and Prithvi didn't seem too convinced.

. . . .

The combined aroma of the room freshener and the scent of his secretary and the respect in the attitude of his coworkers really make the day for the senior editor of the national news channel India news. Daksh's desk as usually got messy as the afternoon passed away and gave way to the beautiful spring evening. The late afternoons and the evenings were certainly the best time in the spring seasons. Though it was not the typical spring season like in the country side, this area was far more polluted for a proper spring, the people in the big cities used to call this time of passing winters as the spring season. The desk was occupied by two laptops and one pc and a mass of papers and files that came up in the day. This was the trademark of this cabin, Neena got the office and the table especially, very neat and clean before Daksh took his seat and by the time Daksh left his office it became such a mess that if you had to find out some paper on that table it will be morning by the time you get the paper . . . Daksh kept everything on the table. His pc, his personal laptop, all the files, all the papers, the newspaper cuttings, glasses, even cups of coffee and every other thing you can think of in an office.

According to Neena, Daksh was, by far the best boss, she still remembers her interview when Daksh joined this office. It was her first job interview and she was really nervous. But Daksh had helped her out a lot. He had cracked jokes and made her smile in the most stressed out condition and it was something she could never forget. In the interview he had asked her questions like will she smile at him every time she meets him, give him coffee regularly and some more weird stuff, and she easily answered those questions . . . she loved him and adored him. A jolly, fun loving guy, who had a word for everybody was liked by almost everyone. He was very friendly and she liked sharing things with him, Daksh on the other hand, did obviously like her . . . she was insanely hot and sincere . . . and somehow she had some magic which made the coffee machine's regular coffee tastier . . .

'But first things first . . .' he thought to himself as he distracted himself from her and got back to the piece of news that was to be relayed next hour . . . 'I sometimes wish I could get my life back . . .' he thought as he looked at the photo of Charvi that was his desktop background . . . he was definitely attracted to hot women but at the same time he had immense love for his wife . . . he sighed and started working on the piece of news . . . There were many things on his mind . . . . And there seemed to be no way out of the current problem . . . the more he thought about it, the more desperate he felt . . . And he did not want to share it with anybody either . . . it was in his nature . . . he was a very secretive guy . . . many people believed he was shallow and emotionless person with no feelings whatsoever . . . . But very few actually knew that he had a lot of emotions in himself . . . he just didn't let them rule him . . . he believed in reason and allowed his mind rule his heart . . . And except Charvi, he had never given allowed his heart to make a decision . . .

'If only once I can get out of this . . . . I will leave this country forever never to return . . .' But that seemed too farfetched given the current situation . . . life is amazing . . . it gives you many things and take way many things . . . and we humans are always after the things that we don't have . . . He remember he once met a victim of bomb blast a couple of years ago . . . the poor woman lost her husband and her son and left hand was amputated . . . at the age of 32 that poor woman watched her family burn . . . she wasn't able to contain herself with the emotions . . . she kept crying and crying and crying . . . . And finally 2 days later, she committed suicide . . . jumping off the roof of her house . . .

And it was later found out that these terrorist attacks were actually an inside job . . .

Another incident that touched his heart was last year . . . when a minister was passing through a city due to which all the roads were blocked . . . and in that roadblock was an ambulance carrying a 3 month old child . . . who was in an urgent need of medical care and died because of the delay . . . the mother went in a deep shock as she saw her 3 month old child die in front of her very eyes . . .

Another incident was when the bridge to a teerth sthal collapsed under the weight of the bus . . . again 40 innocent people . . . people having families . . . died . . .

Another incident which he covered was the riots . . . people from different communities, under the influence of some bloody politicians, burned down houses . . . killing over a thousand people . . . and there were other numerous incidents where politicians ruined families and homes just for a display of power or for their own selfish motives . . . it was in all senses true that politicians were burning down this country and someone will have to take the responsibility to eliminate them . . . it was necessary . . . once what was called the golden bird of the world was now nothing but a poor country with all the money accumulated in very few hands . . . . The population had increased out of bounds on the past century . . . Nothing about this country seemed right . . . . And someone had to come up . . . and though somewhere he wished Anjana Roy was right . . . that she was doing a good job . . . he had to bend his heart and go against her . . . he had to put her down . . . . His conscious was screaming at him but he had no choice . . . his heart told here that he should support her . . . But he never listened to his heart . . . he will set her down . . . given the stakes . . . he would have to bring Anjana Roy down someway . . . even if it meant taking his own life . . . .

. . . .

CHAPTER 8

March 2012 . . . .

THE RECENT EVENTS HAD GIVEN Daksh some hopes to a better life. He was really very happy that after almost 3 months of turmoil, there was a reason to be satisfied . . . otherwise the guilt was starting to consume him . . . but there was one thing that really mystified him . . . Adhiraj's behavior . . . He was convinced in his heart that Anjana Roy had good intentions . . . Even then, Adhiraj was targeting her . . . Was Adhiraj unaware of this fact or he too, like Daksh himself, had some selfish intentions . . . this could very well be a trap . . . But Adhiraj was their friend . . . Adhiraj could be leading them in the wrong direction . . . Or Anjana Roy actually could be an evil genius as the recent findings hinted . . . Daksh had enormous talent when it came to judging people . . . He never had been wrong in the past . . . and now he was in a situation that caused him to doubt his abilities . . . He couldn't digest the fact that everything was happening exactly the way he wanted . . . His experiences told him that if success seems to be coming easier than expected, either your goal is wrong or the path . . . He wasn't worried about Prithvi . . . he knew Prithvi was just a puppet in their hands and would do anything they convinced him to do . . . But Adhiraj was extremely sly and dexterous . . . He thought about everything since the start, when Adhiraj was showing reluctance for support, under the name of his know-how, his experience . . . Daksh had convinced him, with help from Prithvi, that they could make, if not much, just a little difference . . . Adhiraj, after all his tantrums had agreed to work with them, given the condition that they won't ask him to reveal his sources and also, would work in a very neat methodical manner. Everything seemed alright till then . . . Oh God . . . Everything seemed so perfect . . . flawless . . . but this isn't how real life is . . . there is one small mistake . . . either by him or Adhiraj . . . And both of these things had very rare chances . . . As much as he knew Adhiraj, he was probably the most solicitous man he had ever known . . . it was highly unlikely that he could make such a mistake . . . .

"What are you thinking baby???" Charvi's sweet baby voice shattered his entire stream of thoughts . . . .

"I was just thinking about how hot you would look in that black lingerie . . ."

"Liar . . ." Charvi blushed . . .

"No, seriously . . . common . . . you got to show it to me today . . . it's been a fortnight since you bought it and haven't tried it even once . . ."

"Acchaaaaaa? Aapko thoda sa bhi samay hai humein dekhne ka?"

'Of course dear . . . you are the love of my life . . . And my life is nothing without you . . . You are the reason of my smile . . . you are everything to me . . . common . . . change fast . . . in the meanwhile, I will bring the best wine we have . . ."

"Awwww . . . aaj tume bada pyaar aa rha hai . . . kya baat hai???"

"Kabhi kabhi apni wife se bhi pyaar kr lena chahiye . . ."

"Acchaaaa??? Go fast and bring the wine . . . a very special night is waiting for you ahead . . ."

"I'll be back in a second . . ."

"And hey . . . bring the rubbers from the top drawer in the store room . . . I would love to have some strawberry tonight . . ." So saying she bit her bottom lip and arched her neck slightly . . . and he ran faster than the bullet train . . .

. . . .

Daksh's house, next day.

"Let's get the picture clear, Anjana Roy is the wife of a politician in the Alliance, the current opposition. She is pointing fingers at everyone in BJHP on the ground of corruptions and also some of the ministers in Alliance, while her own husband is a corrupt." Daksh said.

"I think her objective is pretty clear. She is trying to dissolve the central government by creating an uprising. The uprising will benefit the Alliance in two ways, first the central government would dissolve and there would be re-elections, and second BJHP would lose major public support, and as a result Alliance would win in the re-elections." Adhiraj nodded.

"So you mean to say this whole scenario, the whole movement, also called the fight for second independence is actually a major conspiracy to eliminate a major national political party." Prithvi said with a straight face.

"From the current picture of the situation, the answer to your question, is yes." Adhiraj looked Prithvi dead in the eyes.

"Well I agree with Adhiraj on this one." Daksh said convinced.

"Well then we need a plan. We have to stop this. Because if we allow this to happen, then the situation could get worse from where it is now. I mean forget a corruption free country. We might be in a threat of a major crisis here." Prithvi said all cool and composed.

"Yes . . . we need a plan . . . and that too very fast . . . because given her current speed, Anjana would be successful in her endeavors in a month or two." Daksh looked at Adhiraj.

"Well your calculation is right. Because though there are parts in the country where people have lost faith in Anjana, there are also many parts of the country where people have lost faith in BJHP. The idea of re-elections is picking up pace." Adhiraj said in concerned voice.

"What do you suggest?"

"Well we need to stop her. And for that we need to expose her."

"Yes, but if you want to expose her, you will need solid proofs of your accusations. What we have right now won't be sufficient." Prithvi said.

"Yes you are probably right. We have time and material for one and only one blow. And that one blow has to be so strong, that it will destroy her from the very roots."

"Is there any chance that your party get her assassinated?" Daksh interjected in between.

There was a moment of silence and both the friends looked at Daksh stunned. Nobody had expected such a suggestion from him.

"Are you out of your mind???" Prithvi almost yelled. "We are not murderers . . ."

"Hmmm . . . I didn't see that one coming . . ." Adhiraj sighed. "Anyways, that's not an option. Because the moment we assassinate her, people's belief in her would grow exponentially."

"I know, but, an army, no matter how strong, in nothing without a king. They might get angry for a few days or weeks but they won't be able to cause any major harm to the current political situation." Daksh ignored Prithvi.

"You have lost your mind." Prithvi slumped back in the sofa feeling disgusted.

"What you are saying is true, but at the same time we cannot eliminate the possibility that someone else won't come and stand in her place. She has inspired thousands of people to do something for their country. Killing her would just strengthen their belief in her, and definitely would give Alliance a major upper hand on BJHP. Remember, she is a part of Alliance. Do you think they would take the falling of their Ace so easily? There would be another uprising, and another people's guardian Angel would emerge. Kill that one and there would be another one . . . How many do you think we can kill??? No . . . there is only one way out of this, and that is, expose her and set her down once and for all. No other way." Adhiraj said.

"Thank you Adhir for talking some sense into this idiot." Prithvi sighed.

"Well Prithvi, I know what I am saying. You don't understand the criticality of the situation. These are desperate times." Daksh said angrily to Prithvi.

"No time is so desperate that you have to take some good person's life." Prithvi argued back.

"That's what I am saying . . . you don't understand the situation we are in." So saying Daksh got up and went into the kitchen to grab some alcohol.

Adhiraj looked as he went . . . he knew Daksh was hiding something . . . And he knew Daksh well enough to know that what he was saying would have a very rational explanation from his point of view . . . He was seeing Daksh desperate for the first time . . . . Back in school days, when Daksh was a small kid, even then Daksh won't say something as irrational or impractical thing as he did today. 'Dada . . . work fast . . . before he does something that we all would regret . . .' Adhiraj prayed in his mind . . . He had to unerstand what was going in Daksh's mind . . . and for that he had to know what had transpired in Bhopal . . . and the clock was ticking . . . there was no time . . .

. . . .

January, 2012, Bhopal.

"Once we crack this one, no cricketer will ever dare to indulge in match fixing." Anil smiled as he and Daksh rode in the news channel van.

"Yes . . . cricket is considered to be the religion of this country . . . . And these players play with the sentiments of people when they sell themselves to gangsters and rookies. Today we will finally have something against them."

"Who are these people we are exposing today sir?" The third and the last person in the van, Rachna, said with an excitement in her voice which she tried to conceal but failed.

"You ever heard of gangster Raman Ahuja?"

"Yes sir."

"And the all-rounder Mayank Sharma?"

"Yes sir. But Raman Ahuja is the biggest gangster in the state sir, and has his connections with the very top people in the country sir . . . including chief minister of several states . . . aren't you scared . . . I have heard he kills anyone who steps in his way."

"Hahaha . . . I know . . . But I am not scared of anybody . . . and you should not be either . . . if he has national connections, we are a national news channel . . . people should be scared of us . . . Well anyways, Raman Ahuja is going to meet Mayank Sharma in the hotel Dolphin in an hour. And Raman Ahuja is said to have crores of rupees at stake in the World cup final next week. So it is very obvious that Raman Ahuja isn't meeting Mayank Sharma so secretly to wish him best of luck for his game . . ."

"Yes sir . . . But how did you know that they are going to meet sir?"

"You are new Rachna so I am giving you an advice . . . never ask a reporter about where he gets his inside information . . . The less you know such people the better . . . You are accompanying us for the first time so it's okay . . . but don't ask again . . ." Daksh smiled . . .

"Okay sir . . . sorry . . ."

"Hey it's okay . . . you will learn soon . . . . Everybody does with time . . ." Daksh winked at her. "Anyways . . . we are booked in room number 413, and they are meeting in 404. Rachna you will go first and change in the room service clothes fast . . . meanwhile I'll distract the people around . . . Anil break in the room 404 and plant the cameras . . . and be careful . . . we don't need to caution them."

"Got it . . ."

"And if everything goes as per the plan, there's a party in for you two . . . go kids . . . make me feel proud . . ." So saying Daksh got off the van and indulged in his work . . .

. . . .

January, 2012. Jaipur.

"Where is the Inspector Prithvi Singh Chauhan of the police station?" DIG Ratan Singh roared on the telephone.

"Sir, he got an information about a major drug deal in the city. He, along-with 7 other policemen, has gone to break the deal and arrest the mafias." The constable shivered as he replied.

"Why was I not informed about it?" Ratan Singh was infuriated.

"I don't know sir. I don't have anyy idea where he is or who he is going to arrest."

""Tell him to contact me as soon as he returns . . . and I want the file about today's arrest on my desk before the day is over. Do you understand?"

'Yes sir. I'll inform him."

"And if doesn't return in 1 hour, inform me. And, again, he is to call me as soon as he returns, it's a very important matter, and if it doesn't happen, I will fire you."

"Okay sir . . . I will . . ." The constable kept the receiver with shivering hands . . .

'God knows what he has done now . . .' the constable thought to himself . . . he knew that his senior gets into a lot of trouble for doing the right thing . . . he just wished he was okay . . . where ever he was . . . .

. . . .

CHAPTER 9

A couple of days later . . .

"So what is your plan?" Daksh asked in a hurried voice.

"Well we know the truth about her." Adhiraj said.

"Partial truth." Prithvi interjected.

"Yeah I know . . . the plan is simple . . . we just use her tactics on her."

"What do you mean?"

"We accuse her. In a proper press conference we ask her straight."

"But don't you think that would bring us in light. Plus that would raise a whole lot of questions."

"Well we use BJHP's shoulder for that."

"How?"

"We tell the partial information to Rajaswamy Mohan and let him deal with it. I know Rajaswamy Mohan. He can make a mountain once he gets a pebble." Adhiraj grinned.

"Well this idea seems good. What do you say?" Daksh looked at Prithvi.

"I agree. This way, no one amongst us would be highlighted and our objective would be completed too." Prithvi replied.

"So how much time do you think all this will take?' Daksh looked at Adhiraj.

"I'll talk to Rajaswamy first thing tomorrow morning and then let him proceed. That's my 2 cents. What do you guys say?"

"Yes . . . this sounds okay . . . we don't hurry and let the best man in the field take over." Prithvi said with a smile.

"Hmmm okay . . . it seems right . . . What do we do in the meantime?" Daksh said.

"For now . . . we go back to our daily routine . . . Get out of the spotlight. I don't want anyone to suspect any of us. We have been poking around for quite a while now."

"Yes I agree. So it's done then. We do as Adhiraj says and stop peeking here and there. We don't want to attract attention of any sort." Prithvi said.

"Well I guess you two are right. I just don't want that Anjana Roy get away clean. I hope you understand my concern." Daksh said.

"Don't worry . . . . Rajaswamy will see to it." Adhiraj said with a smile.

. . . .

Next morning, BJHP party office.

The sun shone brightly through the parted blinds. And as usual the medium sized but neat and sophisticated office was filled with a tense air. Rajaswamy Mohan, though was extremely calm and collected, he was sensing the urgency of the situation his legacy was facing. The scenario had changed completely. What started as a small voice against corrupt ministers with some bill had turned into a political war where his entire standing was at stake. He was definitely running out of the small tricks that saved him and his associates on every occasion. He realized that he should have dealt with the matter when it was just a spark. He didn't, and now that spark had resulted into a wild forest fire that was burning down every nook and corner of his kingdom. He knew there were traitors in his party too, who wanted to throw him over and prevent his son for becoming the next prime ministerial candidate, a secret which unfortunately came out a lot before he had anticipated. Anyways, it's never too late, he thought. Just one small straw, and he would survive these high tides. Adhiraj had asked to see him at the earliest, and he hoped Adhiraj had something, he was one of the very few people Rajaswamy trusted. Adhiraj knocked and entered in with a genuine smile and pride in his eyes, an attitude that was certainly reflected in his body language and filled Rajaswamy with hope. Seeing him Rajaswamy Mohan gave him the artificial polished smile that had created misconceptions in minds of many since his very first day in his political career. He signaled him to sit in the chair opposite to him with his eyes.

Even after the composed personality of the great politician sitting in front of him, Adhiraj sensed the uneasiness in his body language. And though somewhat intimated in his enormous confident presence, Adhiraj managed to keep himself together. He is certainly getting worried, though he still had that usual smile outside, so many years of working together gives you an idea when your boss is upset. And this was the feeling that rushed through his mind, and the thought that he had the key to his problem filled him with excitement, because whatever the relations be, he had enormous amount of respect for Rajaswamy as a great leader and politician, and he certainly acknowledged the fact that he was one of the highest minds in the country, "Good afternoon sir . . ." Adhiraj started.

"Good afternoon son . . . . How are you?"

"I am good sir. You look a little bit tense . . . ."

"Hahaha . . . yes son, I am a bit worried. Ms. Anjana Roy is doing an excellent job and as a result our livelihood is at stake. So I should be a little worried. You tell me. How did you come today?"

"Sir I think I have the key to our solution . . . ."

"Yes??? Please go ahead. Tell me what you got."

"Well I have been doing a bit of research on Anjana Roy, as you know, its my forte" Adhiraj said with a bit of a smirk, "you know, who she is and why is she doing all this?? And I came across something interesting."

"Well we know she is a social activist and she is working for the betterment of the country. She is blaming the political parties and challenging their actions. Anything else?"

"No sir Anjana Roy is no social activist. Anjana Roy is a fake identity. She is nobody other than Vijaykant Desai's wife, and this whole stuff is nothing but a well-planned political conspiracy to overthrow the central government, and create a situation of re-elections, and as a consequence eliminate our party once and for all . . ."

"Are you sure of what you are saying? Because your accusation is as bizarre as Anjana Roy's movement." Rajaswamy smiled.

"Yes sir, if you want you can confirm yourself." Adhiraj showed him a red colored file that he had brought. "Anjana Roy, aka Sunanda Vijaykant Desai, was married 26 years ago in a Lucknow, Uttar Pr1adesh. There are the 2 pictures from that marriage that I could get hold of, plus there are some more pictures of her and Vijaykant attending functions together. Reportedly they had a feud some 6 years ago because of which they approached the court for divorce. The court turned down their plea and they have been living separately since then. Apparently it was all a set up to prove the world that they had nothing in between them except hatred, and so, even if somebody raised questions of her alliance with Vijaykant, they could show that there was nothing between the two of them anymore."

"That's amazing Adhiraj, I am proud of you son. I think you have hit the weak nerve." Rajaswamy smiled inspecting the photographs placed in front of him on his table.

"It's very simple sir, a woman of 52 years, who doesn't have a history of even a single social work at any known level, suddenly launches a national movement against the strongest party in the history of this country and then when on denial of her demands she uses the secrets that are known only in the political family is bound to raise doubts."

"Yes you have a point. We should have thought of it before. A lot of damage could have been avoided. Anyways excellent job Adhiraj. So what do you think you are going to do now?"

"Thanks sir . . . . It was just my duty. I will leave it to you if you don't mind. You know how to take the necessary action and our keep the party and its integrity intact. It's very important for me that our party stays the way it is."

"Hahaha . . . yeah I know . . . . many of us are like family . . . . isn't it?"

"Yes sir a lot more than just a family" Adhiraj replied with a sigh and an emotion that his voice tried to hide but that the eyes betrayed "By the way sir, I had a request."

"Yes what is it???"

"Can you please keep our exchange a secret?"

"Yeah definitely, son, it goes without saying. And one advice to you son. There is a cop that has been recently transferred here via special orders from someone on the inside of the central politics and he is digging stuff that should remain buried. Beware, I don't want you to land into trouble of any sorts. So just be on a look out and maintain your low profile."

"Who is it Sir?" Adhiraj said with a concern . . . in the back of his mind he had almost guessed the name but prayed with all his heart that he was wrong."

"His name is Prithvi Raj Chauhan."

"Are you . . ." Adhiraj stared at him but was interrupted in the middle of his sentence. All the while he was told that Prithvi was sent here due to a promotion and not due to political contacts.

"Yes I am sure, and I know you have a dozen questions in your mind. I know about you three and that's why thought of warning you. You should be very careful with people whom you trust."

"What do I do now?"

"For the time being, we don't know his real intentions or who is pulling his strings, so continue things the way they are going now. Remember, he should not have the slightest of doubts that you know this thing."

"Okay sir . . . I'll keep this in mind."

. . . .

"Job done . . . The news is in Rajaswamy's ears, and definitely none of us is in the light." Adhiraj said on the phone.

"That's good. Now I think I know what will your party members do. I want you to keep an eye on the internal activities of the party, meanwhile I would keep an eye on Anjana Roy's activities and Prithvi is digging around for the political connections of Anjana Roy's major supporters." said Daksh.

"Hey hey hey . . . I thought we had a talk about this . . . no more activates . . . I don't want any activities for now. Just go back to the old regular life. Anyways Rajaswamy will have his best men working on this matter even as we speak. Now we have to stop."

"But we are going so smoothly. Why stop in between. If they haven't noticed us yet they won't notice us in the future."

"Because now Rajswamy knows that I am looking into the matter. He would definitely keep an eye on me. He might even get my phones tapped. He is very paranoid. You can't guess his moves at any point in time. SO for now . . . just go lax . . . don't worry . . . we have done our jobs well, and if anything else comes up, I promise you I'll inform both of you and we will get to work. Alright?"

"Okay . . . if you say so . . . Anyways . . . keep me posted . . ."

"Goes without saying my friend . . . goes without saying . . ." So saying Adhiraj hung up. Getting rid of the driver was the first thing he wanted to do ever since he got a driver. The poor man lost his job in 3 days but was happy as he was given 6 months' salary. Adhiraj loved to drive his cars. That was the one thing he had planned to do in his childhood. Be a street racer . . . drive in illegal street races that were won or lost the hard way . . . . Maybe . . . he would get to do it soon . . . He had the money . . . he was just looking for liberty to spend it. He threw his phone on the passenger seat as he pondered Rajaswamy's warning about Prithvi. Prithvi was pulling some strings in the politics off late . . . but the fact that he was working for somebody on the inside didn't seem to be digested. After all he knew Prithvi to be a man of honor, a simple middle class man who would not understand the complexities of politics, and at the same time, his honor won't let him be a puppet for somebody who would pay him money. Could it be possible that someone was trying to con him . . . just like Adhiraj did . . . It was a rare possibility. Prithvi was smarter than that.

A loud ring on the phone disturbed his stream of thoughts. Absent mindedly he looked at the cell phone lying on the passenger seat. Then he realized, it was his second phone. He looked at it, it was a private number.

"Yeah . . . what have you got?" Adhiraj answered the call. He knew, only three people knew about this phone. And he was expecting a call from only one of them.

"This friend of yours, Daksh, he is a lot more complicated guy than we thought. He hasn't left a trace behind in Bhopal. Very few people knows exactly what happened and those who know, won't open their mouths."

"I know it's not easy, that's why I had put you on the job. Look for those who know about him. There must be someone willing to talk for a cheap price."

"I am trying. It just is taking a bit more time than I thought."

"That's the problem. Time is of the essence here. Keep looking, everybody has a price, and if we are not able to pay it, then prey on their weaknesses, trust me everybody, irrespective of their status or authority or position, has got one . . . I don't care if somebody gets hurts . . . just don't kill them or do any kind of permanent damage . . . rest all upto you. I now you have your ways to get people talk."

"Okay . . . I'll speed up the process. Maintaining secrecy and speed at the same time is a difficult job."

"Yes I know. By the way, do you have a very trusted man whom you could bet your life on?"

"Are you kidding me. I don't even trust you. Anyways, why are you asking?"

"I needed someone to go to Jaipur. There's another man I need a full report on. And this time, it's a government matter. So can be a bit more difficult."

"Okay . . . I'll see what I can do. What's the name of this man you want to know about?"

"Prithvi Raj Chauhan. I'll fax you everything once I reach home. And listen, our party might be involved, so be extra cautious."

"Okay . . . I'll see what I can do. Bye. I got to go now."

"Bye." Adhiraj hung up and put the phone back inside his pocket.

He reached his house, where his lovely wife was waiting for him with open arms . . . He could sense the end of this political situation was coming near . . . The lost pieces of the puzzle were slowly coming up, the whole picture would soon be clear. As he closed the door of the car after him, she smiled standing at the main gate . . . he just wanted it to end fast, with her and their marriage intact and out of this country.

. . . .

CHAPTER 10

January 2011, Bhopal.

DAKSH SCANNED THE LOBBY ROOF for the cameras as soon as he entered the door, and then very carefully, hiding his face from almost every angle possible, he made his way to the reception. The receptionist was, a very expected, young and beautiful girl, as most of the big hotels have today. Many believe it works like a charm for the guests, and probably it does, because the hotel industry is blooming.

"Hello Sir, how can I help you?" The receptionist with flowing black hair, an ear to ear smile and a blood red lipstick asked Daksh as he approached the desk.

Daksh saw the golden color badge on the left side of her chest, with black letters bearing the name Ms. Shweta.

"Hello ummm . . . Ms. Shweta, that's a lovely name."

"Thank you sir." She smiled with confidence, but her eyes told Daksh that his charm had worked.

"I have a booking here, by the name of Dr. Ranveer Singh. I gave my preference for a room on 4th floor so they gave me 413. Can I have my keys?"

"Just a minute sir. Let me check in the system. Can I see your identity proof Sir?"

"Yes sure. Actually I forgot my driving license in my car. Do you mind of I show my work ID card?"

"Okay . . . I guess that would do for now." The girl was completely falling for Daksh. The hotel rules strictly required people to show proper identification before entering further into the hotel. Daksh showed an excellent forgery of work identification, presenting himself as the senior manager of a national private bank, he gave his relationship status as unmarried that did work in his favor. He knew the girl was attracted to him. He also knew he was one of the rare customers in this hotel, who was both smart and single. So the attraction was pretty much justified. As soon as he got his hands on the key, he disappeared in to the elevator. In the meanwhile, Anil led Rachna through a backdoor and the fire exit to the changing room, where Rachna changed into the hostel staff dress. As she came out of the room, Anil looked at her, and smiled, the first part of their biggest sting operation in the year was complete.

. . . .

A couple of days later, Daksh's office, Monday, morning.

Daksh walked into his office . . . the usual hustle filled the office as people were coming and settling in their desks, the sweet smell of coffee was starting to fill the area as the peon served the first of the many rounds of the day. The usually observant Daksh ignored everything today. He was lost in a world of his own. He was starting to get tense. The press conference was today, and a lot was at stake. His life literally depended on it. The natural human tendency of getting impatient as the final time gets closer was getting on his as well. He hadn't slept well in the last 6 months or so. The inner conflict was too much for him to suppress. He wanted to support Anjana Roy, even after all had happened, his instincts told him that there was a logical explanation for all the evidence they had found. And even the current situation of the evidences didn't prove Anjana Roy's guilt. So his heart still ached to support her. Just like every day he had to kill his inner voice of supporting her and just like every day he cursed himself for going against her. He mulled over his thoughts as he sat down in his chair and broke his stream of thoughts as Neena came in greeting him good morning with her bright smile. The red color of her lipstick reminded him of the day that changed his life. He ignored all the thoughts as he politely responded to her and motioned her to sit in front of him to brief him about the day's events. The innocuous girl reminded him a lot of his wife. And his wife reminded him of the problem he was struck in. He gave one final hard emotional push to himself, braced himself up and decided to find a way out of this situation. There always is a way out of every situation, it just gets easier or harder with the quality of choices you made regarding the matter.

"What have we got for the day?"

"Sir, there is only one important matter that you need to look into, there is a big press conference in the *ramleela maidan* in the evening. BJHP and Anjana Roy. And because you are the one who knows most about this whole scenario, editor sir has asked you to attend from our agency. Rest all is taken care of."

"There is a press conference today? When did this come out?"

"Last night everything was decided, and Rajaswamy's personal secretary called himself to make sure that a very expert and experienced person attend the conference from our company. And because you are the one handling this case and there is no doubt about your expertise or experience, sir, gave your name immediately."

"Alright, I'll attend the conference. That's not a problem. Anything else?"

"Yes sir, just a few files that you need to look into and give your opinion. That's all for today."

"Alright . . . get me a cup of coffee and the files . . . I'll start right away . . . I don't want to be late for the conference or leave any more pending work for tomorrow."

"Okay sir . . . I'll get them right now . . ."

. . . .

Same day, 4 pm, Ramleela Maidan.

There was a lot of hustle and bustle everywhere. Politicians were arriving, police vans filled with armed policemen were arriving, and people were coming in large flocks . . . Anjana Roy wanted to make it public, and Rajaswamy was more than happy to allow it. He knew what was going to happen at the end of the day. Other members of his party and Anjana Roy and her supports were all clueless as to why Rajaswamy Mohan had asked for a press conference at the earliest possible schedule. Their best guess was he would finally make some negotiations that would bring some peace to the country. Members of BJHP were very unhappy because they were kept in complete darkness about everything until the night before. Nobody but Rajaswamy, Adhiraj, Daksh, and Prithvi knew what was going to happen in the conference, which went public this very morning. The policemen were unhappy because they had to work entire night to make sure the security arrangements were perfect. Supporters from both the parties were anxious as to what would happen at the end of the day. Many believed that Rajaswamy had stalled

Anjana Roy enough and it was finally time to get to a conclusion. So as a result everybody was either angry, unhappy or impatient. All but Rajaswamy, who, even with such an expertise to hide all his emotions, was barely able to conceive the smile in his eyes. Finally, everybody got to their respective seats. Rajaswamy eyed the audience. The first two rows were nothing but reporters and press representatives, his eyes met Daksh's for a moment, but both broke it off in an attempt to behave like strangers. Rajaswamy continued his scan, there were a few rows of VIPs behind the reporters and then there was the common public, all of them standing, eagerly waiting for the conference to start and to end, and for the conclusions that would come out. Each hoped that it would turn out good for the people they supported. Many people had come to witness the presence of Rajaswamy Mohan, who was rarely present at such public places. He always maintained his low profile, rarely made public appearances, in the past decade, he never made a public speech, and still, he was the main center of the party, the Prime Minister Rajeev Sinha didn't get the kind of attention or respect that Rajaswamy did. And Rajeev Sinha hated Rajaswamy for this. Rajaswamy had his aura, the most graceful, charismatic figure in the current Indian politics. For some reason, he never became the prime ministerial candidate, and that reason mystified almost everybody who knew him. But as a result of that, Rajeev Sinha, whom Rajaswamy promoted for the seat, held Rajaswamy in high regards. At the end of the day, they disliked each other, but had enormous respect for each other, probably the same kind of relationship between most of the other members of the party. And as a result of the cold war, the internal bonding of the party had started to strain. And this was something Rajaswamy did not like, and the things he didn't like, Rajaswamy eliminated them.

The conference was about to commence, everybody was on the edge of their seats, as the spokesperson, Aranya Dixit took his place behind the microphone, cleared his throat in the anticipation of what might come, took a deep breath, and started . . . .

. . . .

As Aranya Dixit started in the conventional manner, addressing everyone, Anjana Roy sat with a calm smile across the stage. Adhiraj sat in a chair behind Rajaswamy with the anticipation of the things to come. Only he, along with Rajaswamy, Daksh and Prithvi knew where and how this day was going to end. Rajaswamy had trusted no one with this information. It was his ace and he could not risk it. Adhiraj saw Daksh sitting in the very first row with a straight face and an anxious look in his eyes, Prithvi was also there, again with a straight face but a very concerned look in his eyes. Adhiraj then looked at Rajaswamy, who was the very same man he was 9 years ago. Unwillingly he went on a trip to memory lane. It was 9 years ago, but it was as fresh as the memory of the same day. And it had to be fresh, it was the day that changed Adhiraj's entire life. Constant rows with his father had filled him with contempt. His father wanted him to do master's in business and take care of the legacy he built with so much care. But Adhiraj was adamant. He wanted to be a writer. He was extremely creative when it came to make plots and stories and that was the talent Adhiraj wanted to nourish. And finally one day, after a huge row with his father Adhiraj stomped into his room and his father went out. Worried, his mother called their very close family friend, who was a classmate of Adhiraj's father and their families were in close contact ever since. Adhiraj's mother, Swaroopa, explained the whole story and the family friend was more than willing to help. He called Adhiraj to Delhi and with his best resources, trained him to use his plot making skills and creativity in real life politics, and also promised him that sooner or later, he will give Adhiraj a chance to fulfill his dream of being a writer. While Adhiraj's father was more than happy to see his son take up a proper career, he was also worried about his wellbeing in politics. But Swaroopa convinced him about the brilliance of their family friend, who was more than capable of taking care of Adhiraj. The relationship of Adhiraj and his mentor was a secret till date, a secret known only to the four people, Adhiraj, his parents, and the godfather himself.

Adhiraj's stream of thought was broken as he heard the roar of round of applause, which was louder than the thunder, Adhiraj looked up to see Rajaswamy slowly and gracefully rising from his seat and walk up to the dais. He commanded that respect, that authority. The unmistakable charisma and extremely self-confident personality that forced even the enemies to look at him with respect. He wore a white kurta pyajama that was white as the feathers of a swan, clean shaved, neatly combed hair that were now the same color as his dress, and the black chappals and a brown shawl draped over his shoulders. He started speaking, in that typically calm way of his, very slowly and deeply, never raising his voice above a certain pitch and volume, as if every word was processed in his mind before coming out of his mouth, as if each word he spoke was extremely important, he raised his hand to crowd, which fell pin drop silent in moments . . . . It didn't matter whom you supported, everybody was eager to hear Rajaswamy speak . . . he rarely did, but whenever he did, it changed the entire face of the situation.

"Bhaiyo aur beheno . . . . Sabhi ko Rajaswamy ka namaskar . . . hum, puri party ki taraf se, aapko dhanyavaad dete hai ki aapne hum par bharosa kiya aur humein vote dekar aapki seva krne ka mauka diya. Par abhi haal hi mein, kuch galatfehmiyo ka shikaar hokar, Anjana behen humse thodi naraaz ho gyi thi . . . Aur kyoki janta bhi unhi ke samarthan me thi, aur janta ki iccha thi ki hum unki iccha ko maan le, toh humne socha ki kyo na janta ki baat maan li jaaye. Aakhir hum janta k sewak hi hai, janta ka aadesh toh maan na hi padega . . ."

Hearing him, a smile came across Anjana's face, but not the one that had contentment, the smile had anticipation, as if she was expecting some kind of a blow from Rajaswamy. Adhiraj noticed it but couldn't digest it. Rajaswamy continued . . .

"Hum Anjana behen ki maangien puri krte hai, bas hamari ek shart hai."

Saying so he looked at Anjana Roy, who nodded affirmatively but didn't say anything.

"Jab ye bill pass hoga, aur aapne jin gine chune mantriyo pr ilzaam lgaya hai, unke saath saath dusre bhrasht netaao ko bhi saza di jayegi. Fir bhale hi who aapke pati hi kyo na ho . . ."

As soon as he finished his sentence, the whole crowd and everybody else on the stage started whispering . . . some out of confusion, others out of curiosity . . . while Anjana Roy, continued with her smile . . .

"Bhaiyo, beheno, shayad aapko pata nhi hai, hamari Anjana behen, ya mai kahu, Leelawati behen, ke pati aur koi nhi balki alliance party ke neta, Vijaykant Desai hi hai. Khair, is baare me baat chit toh hoti hi rahegi, muhje lgta hai ki Anjana behen ko is shart ke baare me sochne k liye thoda waqt chahiye. Bahut bada faisla hai behen, jitna waqqt chahiye le sakti ho . . . Aaj k liye ye sabha yahi samapt ki jaaye, hum sabhi ko bahut saare dusre kaam bhi hai . . ."

So saying Rajaswamy folded his hands to a crowd that stared at him or Anjana Roy in utter disbelief . . . There was murmuring . . . there was confusion . . . The confusion turned into panic, and the panic gave way to anger . . . the supporters who had the tremendous faith in Anjana Roy couldn't take the new information very well. They started rioting and advancing towards the stage. Anjana Roy remained very calm and maintained her smile as Prithvi and a couple of other policemen rushed to her to escort her out safely, while some rushed to Rajaswamy and his group. The rest were trying to control the angry crowd that was getting wilder and scarier with every moment. Soon there were explosions of tear gas as the police jeeps carrying the important dignitaries exited through a safe route behind the ground.

Adhiraj had noticed every move of Anjana Roy, and was mystified with the composure she had maintained. Her entire game was blown into pieces . . . years of hard work and planning had failed in one single moment and she still seemed pretty much calm. It meant only two things, either she had accepted the reality and decided to behave like a mature individual . . . or she had a game plan . . . Though the first option seemed really unlikely, he with all his heart hoped that it was the first option. He looked at his dada, who understood what he wanted to say, and in return gave a very assuring look, just like he had been giving in the last 8 years . . . his dada, his godfather . . . was a great man indeed . . . .

. . . .

CHAPTER 11

January 2011, Bhopal.

Daksh, saving his face from the cameras as best as could, inserted the hooked end of a paper clip in the keyhole and applied a slight tension to the right hand side. Then, he inserted the straight end of a second paper clip just below it, feeling the tumblers in the lock. "I wish I had my tools to break this lock." He said as he struggled to find the right spots. They needed a card and a key at the same time to open the door, Anil, while stealing the uniform of the hostel staff from the laundry, also stole the master cards that were allotted to the room cleaners. Unfortunately, the keys weren't kept in the laundry room and so Daksh had to pick the lock with the paper clips. Rachna was nearby, pretending to clean a large flower vase kept outside the room, while providing Daksh the necessary cover, and in full of admiration for her boss, while Anil was at the gates, looking for anybody coming in their direction. Clearly Rachna had never seen anybody pick a lock so smoothly before. She couldn't take her eyes off Daksh, who was fully engrossed at the job in hand. Suddenly, there was a very, very faint click as the tension of the paper clips gave way and there was another click of the lock opening. Rachna then punched the card and the door opened, Daksh grinned with pride as he looked back on his days on the street where he had learned all this stuff. He got in and while Rachna stayed outside at the door and Anil kept the guard. He unzipped the small bag he was carrying with him and took out two small cameras. He then skimmed the entire room and chose two spots that practically covered the whole room. He looked at the cameras and for a moment gazed in wonder at the amazing work of scientists and engineers. 6 years ago, when he had started his career, such things were not so easily available, and now a days, engineering had progressed at a stupendous rate, and achieved things that seemed impossible just a decade ago. Now a days, a sting operation was really facilitated with this kind of technology. He checked his black colored digital wrist watch . . . it was almost time . . . Raman Ahuja would be checking in in the hotel soon . . . he checked the on switch on the cameras and moved out, locked the rooms the same way he had unlocked them and then entered his room 413 diagonally opposite to 404, and turned on the TV and switched on the music channel. He was soon joined in by Rachna and Anil.

"Sir why did you ask me to wear this uniform? I mean the plan that we have does not require any need of a staff member."

"I know Rachna, but our plan solely depends on how they do their dealing. So if they make any changes, we will have to as well. We cannot leave any lose ends. As a member of the staff, you are a part of the hotel. You can move around unnoticed, blending in with the environment. You are practically invisible. People notice your presence but they don't mind it. You could even knock on their door on the pretext of room service and carry out the job effectively."

"Oh yes right. Now I know why they call you brilliant. All your operations are first class. No chance of failure." Rachna smiled with admiration.

"Hahaha . . . . I guess that's enough buttering for the day. I guess we need to pass the next hour waiting for them to finish their deal and exit the hotel. It was going to be one of the biggest sting operations of his life till date. Though Daksh was not fully satisfied . . . he had to pick Rachna instead of Aarti, his friend who called in sick this morning, and recommended Rachna. He didn't trust Rachna very much, after all he hadn't known her for long, and he had never worked with her. She seemed innocent though, but this was the problem, she seemed really innocent and talked really sweet . . . and he knew the people who looked innocent and talked really sweet can never be trusted and so he had always avoided them. But still here he was . . . with one of those so called good and innocent people, in what was the biggest evening of his life. This would bring him more name, fame and money making opportunities than all the operations combined that year. It just had to succeed. Somewhere he had a deep feeling . . . a feeling of uncertainty, a rare feeling, and he didn't like that feeling. Because it stopped him from feeling happy, from feeling contented. And as a consequence of this, he started wishing that the time should pass faster . . . it had brought him to a point where he just wanted to get it over with, unlike the other times when he savored every moment. This operation was really different. It was big, and it was super smooth, and it didn't make him feel good . . .

. . . .

January 2011, Jaipur

"We will be all over the news . . ." Rajan Goswamy said getting in the driver seat of the police van.

"Yeah . . . after all that's what we want . . . isn't it?" Prithvi smiled as the van started and turned it towards the Ram Vilas chowki, where Prithvi was posted as the senior inspector and Rajan Goswamy was the sub inspector and a very good friend. They had known each other for 3 years now, had a very similar mentalities, accompanied each other on many take downs such as the one they had earlier that day, and they had saved each other's life on more than one occasion. As a result their professional relationship had turned into a friendship they both favored. Just like politics, police was also a profession where you couldn't trust many people.

They were cracking jokes and laughing . . . the mood was good. They had just taken down a group of drug dealers and that too with a lot more ease than they expected. The party selling the drugs didn't have many arms with them, and the party buying them was too high to do much damage. All were arrested, 7 people in all, all males, ranging from ages of mid-thirties to teenage. Now it was party time for Prithvi and Rajan as they reached the chowki. Little did they know that an adventure was awaiting them. As he entered the chowki, he was greeted by the constable to informed him about the call from DIG Ratan Singh. Ratan Singh, was the only senior officer who liked Prithvi. The rest of the police force wasn't very happy with his honest and proper ways . . . it caused them a lot of trouble as Prithvi Singh never listened to anybody and did things as he saw fit. He immediately called Ratan Singh.

'Hello, Inspector Prithvi Singh Chauhan reporting sir."

""Where were you Prithvi?" Ratan Singh enquired.

"I was taking down a small gang of drug dealers, sir. Since I am forbidden from touching the big fishes, I have to remain content with all this small cracks." He smiled as he heard the sarcasm in his own voice. And it was true, Ratan Singh had warned him about getting into deep with the wrong people who had political connections. Jaipur, though a very peaceful city, was still the capital city, and had a good crime rate and political influence.

"Yes I know. Anyways there's a good news for you."

"What is it sir?"

"You always say you don't get bigger things to do, don't you?"

"Yes Sir."

"Well here is your chance do to something big. I can't tell you much on the phone, visit me right now."

"Okay sir, I am on my way. Can you tell me what is it about? I am getting really excited with sound of your voice."

"It's the central politics son. Somebody is pulling the necessary strings to get you posted in Delhi. This is all I can disclose for now. Come and I'll brief you about everything."

"Alright sir." Prithvi kept the receiver with a smile on his lips and anticipation in his heart.

· · · ·

Present, next day after the conference

The whole country was in chaos. Divisions based on political lines and beliefs were increasing. The entire movement had lost its flow. There were still some people, who wanted to end the corruption in this country and thus the movement still somehow sustained. Other than Anjana Roy, there was a small bunch of powerful people who were standing against the central party but the platform, the anti-corruption symbol, Anjana Roy was destroyed. Members of BJHP party felt relieved after almost a year of turmoil . . . the tables were turning. Rajaswamy sitting in his chamber, smoking his usual cigarettes, was waiting for the plan to take full action. According to his prediction, the whole plan had a loophole, and so there would be a little backfire. He came up with another plan to turn that backfire into a platform to eliminate his next threat, the Alliance. He knew after the revolution of Anjana Roy, BJHP was in a critical condition. And alliance would not miss this opportunity. They would make a head on collision. If Rajaswamy survived this, he would definitely cement his position in the center for the decade. Plus there was some dirt in his own party that he had to remove, and make way for his son, who would be coming soon after completing his studies in the United States. He was planning to make him the next President of this country. Everything was in order. Now he just had to take one more step.

And then wait for the Alliance to make a move. So without making any further delays, he picked up his phone, made a call to his favorite and most trusted reporter, and gave him a news that would definitely get the reporter promoted. It went something like this.

'Rajaswamy Mohan, the party leader, after a heated discussion with Rajeev Sinha, has decided to accept the public demands and go for a re-election. He justifies that even though Anjana Roy was a corrupt herself, she was right when she said that there is a lot of dirt in the Indian politics, especially BJHP and Alliance, which are the two leading parties in the nation today. He has also promised that he would take the necessary action, and fire all the members of his party who are found guilty by the supreme court. He says, from now on, there won't be any criminals in his party. He also has made a very sincere request to the Alliance party president, Jayesh Bhandaarkar, to do the same so that we could build a better nation. Now the question is, will Jayesh Bhandaarkar agree? And also, Rajaswamy stick to his claims? Only time will tell. This is reporter Mahesh Singh, from news central."

Rajaswamy smiled when this came out to public. Till now, convincing Rajeev Sinha was the toughest part of their plan. He wasn't ready to give up his chair. But well, Rajaswamy is Rajaswamy, nobody had better negotiation and conversation skills that he did. So it was up. Re-elections in 1 month. Now he had to wait for the opposition to fire.

In the meanwhile, he thought it would be a good time to get Anjana Roy arrested. They had the charges on her, her support was broken, so it was high time he put an end to her days of freedom. He made a call to the commissioner of the Delhi police, Rudra Pratap Singh, a man of dignity and respect in the police force. Rudra Pratap was one of the many high authorities who were under the debt of Rajaswamy. They all had got into trouble at some point in time, and Rajaswamy had helped them. Just when they thought that their careers were over, Rajaswamy would swoop in like a guardian angel, and save them, and demand nothing in return. He did all this in the name of helping good people. As a result of this, many people were now under his thumb. A free favor made them his subordinate allies for life. What people didn't know was that their bad circumstances where created by Rajaswamy himself. When the old commissioner of police was retiring, Rajaswamy realised he would lose a major ally, so he asked for a list of people out of whom, one would be selected as the commissioner. He studied them all and came to a conclusion that Rudra Pratap Singh would be the best choice. So he pulled some effective strings, and some of the deeds of the dark past of Rudra Pratap Singh sprang up. Soon it came to a point where he was on the verge of losing his job. Seeing the ground closing in beneath his feet, Rudra Pratap Singh became desperate. He tried his best but to no avail. Then one day, somebody advised him to go see Rajaswamy. Rudra Pratap was so desperate that he went straight to him and said,

"I'll offer you any price if you could help me keep my job intact, and if possible my promotion. Please help me."

Rajaswamy looked him in the eyes and calmly replied, "I don't do anything for the money. I just do things if I feel I should do them. Money was never my dream. As far as you are concerned, I think you are a good man officer. Go, take a vacation for a week or so. When you come back, I promise your integrity and your promotion would be delivered to your doorstep."

Rudra Pratap Singh was stunned at the turn of events. He managed to stammer, "Thanks a lot sir. Please tell me if there is anything I can do."

"If you really want to do something, go to Dubai. I have heard it's an amazing place." Rajaswamy smiled.

By the time Rudra Pratap Singh returned, everything he was worried about had vanished. Rajaswamy killed all the stories he himself had given birth to, and there he was, Rudra Pratap Singh was now the commissioner of Delhi police and a puppet of Rajaswamy. And just like this, Rajaswamy had gained the gratitude of many high ranking officers in all the departments. They were all at his beck and call.

He made the call to Rudra Pratap, "Rajaswamy here, I guess its high time you arrest Anjana Roy. And you are smart enough to press the right charges. I just want to see her behind the bars, on a lifetime basis."

And Rudra Pratap Singh was more than ready to this job for the man who was the reason of his position and wellbeing today.

. . . .

CHAPTER 12

A few days later . . . Adhiraj's mansion . . .

WITH HIS HANDS FOLDED, ADHIRAJ got on his knees and touched his forehead on the ground, in front of the idol of Lord Hanuman, and murmured the last of his morning prayers. He couldn't start a day off without this. Without the praise of his lord, he felt empty, low at confidence and uneasy throughout the day. So he did his customary puja and just as he was about to join his wife for the breakfast, he received a call from Prithvi.

"Dude, Anjana Roy got arrested half an hour ago."

"Yes I know. I heard. Why are you so shocked? After all, that was our motive, wasn't it?"

"Our motive was to set India corruption free, and not send Anjana Roy into prison. I was just going through her file, and the charges pressed on her are bizarre."

"I know. We had to send her behind the bars on some pretext or the other. And that is how we were going to stop her. She was not a revolutionary bro, she was planted. She had to be taken out. We didn't kill her because that would be wrong, but after all she did, she did deserve a prison sentence."

"Hmmm well somewhere I guess you are right. Anyways, keep me posted. Any plans involving me in the near future?"

"Nope . . . not yet . . . we need to choose a target first. And that has to be done systematically. I'll let you know once we come up with anything."

"Alright then . . . catch you later . . ."

"Bye bro." Saying so Adhiraj hung up. For some reason, he felt that Prithvi did favor Anjana Roy a lot. Like from the very start, he was against their going after her. Once he agreed, he didn't take active part in executing the plans, rather he preferred to sit and watch. And the Prithvi he knew back in the childhood, was a very active kid. Volunteering for almost everything he could get his hands on. Plus, since he learnt about Prithvi's political contacts from Rajaswamy, he had started tracking his past in Jaipur, and there too, as his sources told him, Prithvi was a very active worker. He had suddenly changed after coming to Delhi. So he had to find two things about him, first, the political connections that had helped him to reach at this platform, and second, what caused this change all of a sudden. Because people don't really change. Deep down, they remain the very same they always were. He made a mental note of talking to Rajaswamy about it. In the meanwhile, his lovely wife was waiting with a splendid breakfast, and if there was anything he loved as much as his wife, it was the delicious food she cooked. So there was no sense in keeping the food waiting.

· · · ·

January, 2011, Jaipur.

"I don't get it. Why is she calling me?" Prithvi said with the thrill in his voice, reading the file in his hands. He had admired her ever since the beginning.

"Well as people believe, she has strong political connections. And now, as she has a lot of enemies in the political field, she needs a special person in the police force. But she doesn't trust any of the policemen in Delhi, says they are all corrupt. So the home minister called a meeting last week and asked us to give the name of the best officer of our city. I recommended your name, and, out of 26 names that were submitted, she chose you."

"Wow, this is unbelievable. Thank you, sir. I am more than honored."

"Well it was your hard work Prithvi. She studied all the 26 files carefully, and at the end she chose only you. She says, you have a lot of potential as a police officer, and she can't see such a huge potential go down without being given even a single opportunity."

"Thank you sir. I have always respected her. It would be so great to work with her."

"Yes . . . and I hope your orders are clear to you. You have to protect her at all costs, wherever she is. Her safety is of utmost importance to you, and you have to take every step with caution. You will go as a normal officer there, nobody knows your exact purpose of the transfer, except her and me. Along with you, there are 5 other officers who will be transferred to Delhi, all with different orders, so that nobody suspects anything. I'll give you a copy of files to study them. I'll personally see that all your records be taken from our record room and moved to a safer location, where only me and a couple of other people have access to it. From now on, you are on a very important mission. I hope you do well. Any questions?"

"No sir. I pledge to assist her in any task she asks me to, in any way she asks me to. Her safety is more important than my life."

"Good. You may leave."

"Alright sir."

"And yes, one more thing, she doesn't like titles of any kind. So it would be better if you called her directly by her name, Anjana Roy, she likes to be called directly with that name."

"Got it Sir." Prithvi said with a smile, as he exited the DIG's office with Anjana Roy's file in his hand.

. . . .

People had lost faith. After the fall of Anjana Roy, the so called struggle for second independence was on the deathbed. Rajeev Sinha had mixed feelings about the matter. He was very happy with the way Rajaswamy had saved the day, but at the same time he was very upset to resign from the prime minister's post, and hold re-elections. Though he somewhat Rajswamy to ensure their party's victory, but you never know, politics is a game of uncertainties. One good move by opposition and you are dead meat. But he still consoled himself as he got into his white Mercedes. He felt a little bit different today in his car, like something had changed. But he had a ton of different things on his mind to worry about. He had to go to the adjacent city, and wanting to finish his work quickly, he asked the driver Ram Prasad, to go from the short cut and not the long highway. The short cut wasn't a very good road, but it was deserted, and plus, living in India rarely provided the luxury of good roads. So he decided to take the deserted road. As they were almost half way through, Rajeev Sinha heard a faint beep. The sound of the car moving on the rough patch of the road made it hard for him to hear it properly, but he was sure, it was a faint beep, and within moments he realized, the sound was coming from the car itself. He immediately realized the situation, and screamed at Ram Prasad to stop and just as he was about to jump out of the moving car, the bomb exploded . . . .

'This is a very sad time for the entire country, as the today afternoon, 3 hours ago, the prime minister of the country died in a bomb explosion. Prime Minister Rajeev Sinha, was travelling via the link road that connects the two main highways of the city, with two cars of armed forces accompanying him, which however, intact. The prime minister's security in charges have been fired on the spot. They say that the prime minister's car was bomb proof. So the police suspects that the bomb was placed inside the car, which is possible only if the driver Ram Prasad was a part of the whole plan. Ram Prasad, who is also found dead, is the major suspect, however, police has refused to disclose any details of who might have been behind this gruesome murder. The murder could either be a terrorist attack or the dirty politics, we cannot say anything for now. The entire nation, including the family of Rajeev Sinha, and many members of BJHP are still in shock. However with the re-elections 2 weeks from now, the BJHP is infuriated with the murder of their party president Rajaswamy Mohan has requested the high command to provide additional securities to all the ministers of BJHP. He says the death of the party president, and moreover, the country's prime minister is a very shameful act, and whoever is responsible for this can never be forgiven. Now, after repeated requests from the party members Rajaswamy Mohan will hold the post of the party president. This is it for now, we will bring you the latest updates from both the BJHP office and the crime scene. Stay tuned, this is Mahesh Singh, from News central.'

. . . .

The entire nation was gripped in shock at the horrifying event that took place in the afternoon. People still couldn't digest the fact their former president of 12 years was assassinated this afternoon. The news had become international, and the best forces in the country were trying to solve the matter. The only thing that was found till now was the fact that the driver, Ram Prasad was a suicide bomber. The motive and the main brains behind the assassination was still a mystery and Rajaswamy was pressing on harder and harder. The rest of the day passed and the nation started going back to the normal when it received another blow from BJHP. Every news channel was featuring this, Rajaswamy Mohan had accused Adhiraj Goswamy, the leader of the youth force for the BJHP, on the grounds of corruption, and as a consequence of the accusation, had fired him from the party. It was a major blow to BJHP as there were many young supporters of Adhiraj and wanted to see him as a part of BJHP. Later, as Aranya Dixit told the news channels, 'that with the re-elections just two weeks from now, there party was going through their roughest patch. The fact that this is the day when their party president, country's prime minister of 12 years was assassinated and later on, the discovery of their youth brigadier as the center of corruption in their party indeed made this day of January 2013, the black day for BJHP.' And so the day ended. The current situation was very disturbing for the supporters of BJHP. However, the scene was exactly the opposite for a few members of BJHP.

"Hey dada, you are a genius." Said Adhiraj, grinning, as he carressed his wife's hand, who was sitting beside him in the bed.

"So what's the next step?" Adhiraj asked.

"Well for you, it's wait for my command. I'll let you know what you have to do at the time when I need you. For now, you are jobless, so go, enjoy the freedom. You don't have to attend the office from tomorrow. Spend some nice time with Anjali."

"Common Dada, you can trust me."

"Oh common Son, I trust you. I am just bound by my nature of being a very low profile man. I hope you understand. You know how much uneasy it will make me knowing that somebody knows what I am going to do next." So saying, he chuckled.

Adhiraj knew his dada's nature, and he also knew that no amount of convincing can lead to his Dada telling him the secrets. So he bid his farewell for then, and came back to his wife, with whom he was living physically but not mentally for so long . . . . The past few months had been hell, and now finally, today, after such a long time he felt, the love, and the care, and the lust, and the naughtiness coming back. He felt content about his situation, the way he had worked, and content was both the best and the worst feeling in the world. Best because it makes you truly happy, and worst because it kills the drive to move forward.

"So are you done with everything? Because I can't wait to take a bite from you." She said naughtily, looking at him with her bottom lip between her teeth. He looked back at her in the dim light of table lamp.

The dim light had the amazing power to amplify the beauty, be it the dim light of something as abstract as the moon, or something as realistic as the candle, or something as modern as the table lamp, it did the same justice to the fine flawless beauty. And his wife was the most amazing woman he had come across.

"Wow, you look so beautiful," He said with a wink, "I would be more than happy to give you a bite of me," as he leaned into her, and their lips meeting in lust, then passion and then finally abandon.

. . . .

CHAPTER 13

June 2011, Bhopal

ANIL WAITED IN PATIENCE, KEEPING an eye in the corridor. Daksh waited restlessly. The odd feeling was getting to him. Seconds passed like days and minutes like months. It was a while since the two gentlemen, Raman Ahuja and Mayank Sharma, had been in the room 404 for like half an hour now, and the small crew in 413 waited for them to leave the room, so that they could collect their cameras and leave the hotel with the evidence that would take them places. The biggest sting operation in the history of their news agency. It would shake both the underworld and the cricketing world to their core. Maybe this was the reason of Daksh's nervousness. The larger the score, the larger the risk. So Daksh switched off the TV and laid back. Just then Anil spoke up, "Dude, they are leaving." Hearing him, Rachna rushed to the door, to get a glance of the two people. They waited for another couple of minutes as they saw the two gentlemen leave. Anil followed them and found out that Mayank Sharma was staying in a room on the third floor, and so he went to his room, while Raman Ahuja left the building. Anil went down in the lobby and called Daksh to take the cameras and leave the hotel as quickly as possible. Daksh moved swiftly, and along with Rachna, broke into the room number 404 just like he had on the previous occasion, and started looking around the room, for anything else that could have been his evidence. The room was clean, as if, it had been empty all along. Daksh took a deep breath and then looked for the cameras, they were still in their places, and were working properly. 'Thank god, they didn't notice these. Otherwise all the hard-work would have gone to waste.' He thought to himself, and slowly uninstalled the cameras one by one.

Finally, when he took out the second camera, he smiled to himself, thinking he was getting worried unnecessarily, as he looked down at the two small cameras in his hands, the operation had gone down smoothly. He laughed to himself and looked up, and the scene took his laugh and his breath away. There was Rachna standing, with the innocent look in her eyes vanished, a devilish smile on her face, and a pistol in her hand. Daksh smiled at himself, thinking that his gut feeling was, after all, absolutely correct. He looked up at her again, and with a very confident smile, asked her, "What is it that you want?"

"Right now, I just want to kill you." Rachna said with the same devilish smile.

"So, what are you waiting for?"

"She is waiting for my command." The heavy voice echoed in the room, as a 6 feet tall, large, heavy man, dark complexion, French beard and moustache, walked into the room. It was Raman Ahuja.

"I thought you left the building." Daksh smiled at him too.

"Actually, my lookalike did. Talking about me, I never actually entered this room until now. So finally, I have conned the great news reporter Daksh. It's awesome . . . isn't it???" Raman walked in and stood face to face with Daksh.

"Well not yet. I am not giving you these cameras till I am alive. And I am sure you won't make the mistake of killing me here, especially when my friend, Anil is waiting in the lobby for me."

'Who said I wanted these cameras? And who said I want to kill you. If I wanted to kill you, I would have done this long back. But you see, you are my favorite journalist, and I don't eliminate my favorites. And as far as this camera goes, you can show it on the TV whenever you want, it just has the recording of the planning of a charity function after the final match. Sir Mayank Sharma, will donate his entire earnings for the welfare of the people, through me. So the telecast of this camera recording will make us heroes."

"I don't understand. My man never gives me the wrong information. So there was never going to be a match fixing deal?"

"Ahh my friend, don't look so confused. I'll explain everything to you from the beginning. My friends and I have Rupees 200 crores on the line for this match. So we decided to put in some extra money, you know, as safety deposit, on our star player, Mayank Sharma. We decided everything. Now as I said, you are my favorite. You don't leave any scam you get your hands on. So there's a small bug in your office, and every private thing that is discussed there, is heard by Rachna, who, in turn, informs me. So last night, when you two, were planning this sting operation, Rachna, heard you. So I just modified our plan a little, shifted the meeting to room number 304 instead of 404, and kept the room 404 for you exclusively. We knew you would need a third person for this operation, who, as usual would be Arti, so we threatened her to call the day off, and when she did, the next person you could take was Rachna." Raman said slowly yet strongly, while Daksh digested the entire scene.

"Well, what can I say? I always believed Rachna was a very sweet and innocent girl. I never thought she could turn out something like this."

"You see Daksh, this is the mistake everybody does. Innocence is the best camouflage, and innocent people are the most hazardous. You know why? Because innocent people, or people who pretend to be innocent are always underestimated and ignored. And it is always the underestimated potential that comes straight out and punches you right in the face, just like Rachna did to you right now."

"Hmmm . . . . So what do you want from me?"

"I . . . . want you."

"I didn't get you."

"I want you to work for me. I'll give you loads of money, a great reputation, and you will work according to me."

'What if I refuse?"

'You see Daksh, I don't like refusals. I go crazy when somebody refuses me for something. I then use the information about them to destroy them from the very core. You see, I never killed a man who wanted to live. I have killed almost 50 men, and trust me, they all begged me to kill them. I don't kill straight away. Killing is not fun. Keeping them alive, is what punishes people. You know once there was this man, a policeman, who tried misbehaving with my innocent sister, who was returning from the college. Fortunately, before he could do any damage, my men reached the spot, and captured him. I came to know that he too has a sister, and a wife too. So I got the two women kidnapped. We tied him, and made him watch the two women he loved the most, getting raped, by 26 men, for 4 hours continuously, till they passed out. He shouted, swore tried to free himself, while I laughed and my men fucked. For the next week, we gave the three people good food and everything they needed, except clothes for the two women, my men, came in raped either or both the women at their will at any time of the day. After a week was over, their naked pictures and videos were flowing in the market.

After a week, the man humbled, his swearing turned into begging, begging me to have mercy on him and kill him. And when I could no longer see his plight, I did him the favor and killed him. And then I released the two women, who immediately committed suicide."

Daksh stared open mouthed with pure horror in his eyes. How can a man be so heartless?

Raman read his thoughts, and laughed. "This is India son, here the laws apply only to common people, and not the criminals or politicians. We have a green card to do whatever we want. Well anyways, now you see, I don't like being crossed. So you will work for me, my brother actually, he lives in New Delhi. You have to work for him. And don't worry, he would pay you more than you want. As I said, you are my favorite reporter, and so I want you to be paid well. After all, you are now becoming corrupt officially, by joining hands with me and my brother. You will earn a lot. Now go, Anil must be waiting for you. And don't forget the innocent Rachna, she is, after all, a part of your crew."

"But who is your brother? Whom am I going to work for now?"

"Tomorrow, I'll call you and tell you everything. Till then, start packing for Delhi. You leave next week."

So saying Raman went and slumped down on the bed, and Adhiraj left the room in a daze, Rachna accompanied him. In a matter of moments, his life had changed entirely. Only one question surfaced on his mind, who was the elder brother???

. . . .

Present . . . Daksh's office, morning.

Daksh entered his office, everything about the office was usual. The aroma of the freshly made coffee, staff members arranging there papers in their cubicles, seniors giving orders to juniors, a few people who came in his way greeting him. He reached his cabin and saw Neena sitting outside, with the usual smile missing. She greeted him and said that he was called in urgently. He entered his cabin and was shocked to find his boss sitting in the visitor's chair, and a new man sitting in his, the new man, wore a proper executive suit, blue pin striped suit, white shirt, red tie, slightly bald, dark black eyes, fair complexion, slim and slender built, and a not very happy expression on his face. He looked at Daksh, their eyes locked for a moment, and exchanged pure hatred and resentment.

"Daksh", his boss addressed him getting up, "this is Mr. Sai, and he will replace you in this office. You, from today, are terminated. I am sorry, but you need to come with me to fulfill all the formalities."

"But how??? I didn't get a prior notice. On what pretext am I being fired???" Daksh was enraged.

"Well, I guess you are a better judge of that. But I still went ahead, and asked the company to give you 3 months' salary to make up for this. I am bound by the rules Daksh. I have to follow my orders. Come with me. You can complete all the formalities in an hour, then you can leave with your salary."

Daksh knew it was over. He had failed to do the needful and that's why Raman Ahuja had had him fired. And there was absolutely nothing he could do about it, except, accepting his fate, and following his boss to his cabin, and completing everything. He looked at Neena, who was as shocked as he was, and who was as upset as he was, clearly, she did not like her new boss, who could like him. Crankiness oozed out of his pores. But Daksh, had one thing very clear in his mind, if he did not do something quickly, it might be the beginning of his doom. He said a bye to Neena on his way out and then turned his gaze towards the floor, as his colleagues looked at him, some with curiosity, some with pity and some with excitement. And he knew he might have to face a lot more.

. . . .

CHAPTER 14

Present, the Supreme Court.

ADHIRAJ ADMIRED THIS OFFICE. THE furniture was neatly handcrafted from the best British elm available. On the right side of the room there were large cabins that consisted of neatly arranged books about various topics, ranging from the history of law and constitution in India, to the encyclopedias of philosophy and religions and on the left side, was a table that had a classic chess board on it with two sofas on either side. The judge's table was a wooden masterpiece in itself with probably every day to day stationary a part of it. Behind the table, mounted on the wall, were three beautiful paintings. One painting, the one in the middle, particularly caught his attention. It was of a mother feeding her child. Adhiraj was captivated by this painting because the artist had so gracefully depicted the mother breastfeeding her child, probably the most beautiful natural phenomenon among humans for a mother, to look at her child feeding with content. And the unmistakable reflection of love, from the infinite depths of a mother's heart, that is filled with love so pure, that it is beyond the human mind to define in words, it's the same love that makes a mother more gentle than a feather of a dove, and more strong willed that the mightiest of the kings. And the artist had so subtly portrayed this entire phenomena with nothing but pencils, and maybe a black pen at places. And it was so beautiful that Adhiraj lost the track of time gazing at the fine piece of art that he came back to the real world only after being tapped at the shoulder from the large charming man behind him. Adhiraj turned and found the Supreme Court Justice Randhir Singh standing behind him with a broad smile on his face,

"How are you son?"

"I am good dad . . . how are you?" Adhiraj bent down, touching his father-in-law's feet.

Randhir blessed him and looked at the painting Adhiraj was looking at.

"It's beautiful isn't it? I liked it at first sight, and decided to put it in my office. I never took it home, otherwise your mother-in-law would keep it in the house, and you know, after this long in the marital relationship, I really prefer to spend more time at work." Randhir said with a wink as both the men laughed, moving towards their respective chairs, Randhir to the chair behind the table, and Adhiraj to the visitor's chair in the front.

"How is my little girl? I haven't had a talk with her for days now."

"She is doing great dad. Misses you and mom a lot."

"Hmmm . . . well I'll have a talk with her in the evening. Anyways . . . tell me what I can do for my son."

"Well as you know, I was planning to shift abroad, there were some legal formalities in which I need either your advice or help."

"Well I don't see any problems with shifting abroad, if you give the right amount of money to the right people which I believe should not be a problem for you."

"Well actually, I needed two new identities, for Anjali and me."

"I don't understand. Why would you need new identities? I like the names Adhiraj and Anjali."

"Well we like them too. But when Dada's plan is going to execute, we would need to kill the two identities, and thus, close both the files. You know the criminal cases filed against me have really piled up now, and I can't risk anything from my past come into the future. I hope you understand."

"I do . . . alright, I'll help you out. So what is it that you need?"

"I don't want to leave any lose ends. So we will do everything from the basic scratch to the ultimate masterpiece. The two identities won't have a single record of any criminal activities whatsoever, and even if someone wants to dig in their past, they would find that both of them were convent educated, post graduate from reputed colleges, both became orphans, and then had a love marriage. All the details are inside this package. I have put together everything, bank accounts, had a talk with my powerful friends at the schools and colleges. I am just stuck at one thing, I need to get a real passport, not a fake one. And I know you have really strong connections in those departments. So if you could, please get me those two passports. Everything you need is in here, so can I count on you?"

"So now you going to insult me by asking that?"

Adhiraj looked down as he realized that his professional tone had made its way in his personal life. He was just about to apologize when the judge interrupted him.

"Son, you can always count on me. The way you have treated me, if I had a son, he wouldn't have given me that respect, and the way you treat my daughter, she feels like a princess. What more can a man expect? You have me always beside you whenever you need me. Go home and relax. Your work will be done."

"Thanks dad. I'll see you soon." Adhiraj said as they both got up, and Adhiraj touched his feet, before proceeding out of the office.

. . . .

Later that evening, Adhiraj's mansion . . .

Adhiraj sipped his caramel latte as he sat on the sofa switching different channels on the television.

"Life has become really boring for you, isn't it?" Anjali casually walked in and sat beside him on the black leather sofa, with a hand on his thigh.

"Well it won't be after a couple of days. Everybody knows that me and Rajaswamy are sworn enemies. Now I am just waiting for the Alliance to play their move and contact me. And given their current situation, it won't be too long before they get desperate and call me to get to Rajaswamy."

"Yes well, you are playing with the fire, while standing inside a coal mine. I hope you make out of it safely."

"Hey sweetie I will . . . I have enormous faith in dada. His plans always work, and he always wins."

"I know, but try and understand how much I love you. And, love makes us stronger, but our loved ones are our weaknesses too."

"I know baby, I love you too." Adhiraj sweetly kissed the back of her hand.

Adhiraj then looked at the television and a horrifying sight caught his eye, and he almost dropped his mug on the floor, spilling all the coffee. Anjali covered her mouth with one hand, while holding Adhiraj's arm with the other hand. A gruesome encounter had taken place in the slums, just outside the city. The police had raided a huge arms deal, and the smugglers had opened fire, the police retaliated, and in the firing that continued for over 40 minutes, 23 were killed, 11 of which were policemen, and 12 were smugglers, only one smuggler, and 4 policemen survived the encounter. And the thing that shook them was that the encounter was led by the senior inspector Prithvi Singh Chauhan, who, unfortunately, couldn't survive in the crossfire. Now the situation was under control and the entire area was being searched for by the police dogs for any evidence. The chief minister, Rahman Malik was talking about a 'shok yatra' that would go through the heart of the city, to commemorate the martyrs of the city, to let the people know that there were still such people, who were ready to fight for their country, and were not afraid of losing their lives in the process. According to him, 'The shok yatra won't only do justice to the martyrs but also tell the people about their story of bravery, and thus inspire more people to join forces and work for the betterment and protection of the society.' And so it was all set. The entire slum had become a red light area, slowly, the commissioners and the other officers had started leaving the scenes.

Adhiraj was still in shock. Prithvi had died. He couldn't believe the news. How??? Why??? There were so many things going on in Adhiraj's mind. The memories of times that he and Prithvi had spent together. The games they played, the fights they had, all the memories, of their being together, were just . . . memories . . . he so wanted to live them again, but he couldn't. He couldn't believe it was real. Prithvi had just died. His best friend was shot couple of hours ago by some smugglers. He so wanted that someone would come and wake him up, and tell him that it was all a dream, and then the next day he could meet Prithvi and tell him what a stupid dream he had last night. But nobody came, nobody woke him up, it wasn't a dream. He remembered the last time he had a talk with him, it was two days ago, when Prithvi was on his way home, Adhiraj had called him to ask him his whereabouts . . . Prithvi said he was running really busy, but he would make some time this weekend and come to Adhiraj's place for dinner, they would invite Daksh too, along with Charvi, and the three friends and their families could meet again, this time in a little less tense environment. The conversation was still in his mind, and it reminded him of Daksh. 'I should call and inform Daksh', he thought to himself and went for his phone. He dialed the number, and waited for Daksh to answer, every moment that passed sunk him down to the ground of reality, as if the world had slowed down somehow and he could feel the agony, that amplified with every passing moment. The phone kept ringing, but nobody answered, Adhiraj called again, but with the same results . . . Adhiraj tried and tried, but nobody replied. Finally, just when the 7th attempt was about to fail, Daksh picked up.

"Dude, where the hell were you?" Adhiraj almost yelled, the emotions clearly flowing hard and strong in him.

"Hello . . . yes Adhiraj Wassup?" Daksh replied in a deep sunken voice.

Just as Adhiraj was about to continue the conversation, the monotonicity in the sound of Daksh's voice struck him.

"Nothing much here, what's wrong with you?"

"I am doomed bro, I am finished. I am completely finished." Daksh said, holding back a sob.

"What . . . why??? What happened?"

"I lost my job bro. I was humiliated and kicked out. I cannot find a new job, I . . . my life is finished . . ."

"But how? Why?? And why can't you find a new job? You are capable enough."

"It's not about being capable or not. I . . . I just can't . . . . It's a long story, I'll tell you when we meet, and now you tell me, why you called? You called 7 times, it must be urgent."

"Well, I don't know how to tell you this . . . bro, umm . . . Prithvi . . . Prithvi died in a encounter near the slum area . . ." Adhiraj finally let it out with a gasp, ad he knew how it would have struck Daksh, because Daksh was as close to Prithvi as Adhiraj was, and given how upset Daksh already was, it would have killed Daksh to know that one of his closest friends was shot dead at the age of 30.

"How??? How did you know?" Daksh finally managed to speak, between heavy sighs and deep breaths. His voice had become hollow, as if it was dead.

"It's all over the news. Ummm . . . he died a life of a martyr . . ." Adhiraj made a vain attempt at making it sound like it had at least one good side about it. But he knew, it wasn't easy. And given Daksh's condition, he would have to be the one to take hold of the situation, because among the three friends, two now, he was the only person whose life was going as per he had planned.

And so he would have to talk Daksh out of this. Talking had great potential, talking can take you and anybody anywhere you want, but it was not as easy as it seemed. He ended the brief talk with Daksh, and promised to meet him soon, the next day itself if possible, but Daksh seemed adamant, so Adhiraj bid his farewell and hung up. He looked at Anjali, who was calling Prithvi's home to talk to his wife, to console her, he gave a slight smile as he looked at her, a smile that tried to hide the million emotions that were running through his mind. But now there was nothing he could do, because he knew Daksh was in deep with the wrong people, and if he tried to help him in anyway it might take a serious toll on the road to his dream.

. . . .

CHAPTER 15

Next day . . . Adhiraj's mansion.

'HEY BHAGWAAN . . . YE KAISI DUVIDHA *hai??? Ek taraf mere dost hai . . . aur ek taraf mera sapna . . . meri madad kar . . . Nahi toh mai barbaad ho jaunga . . . dhanyavaad . . .'* Adhiraj finished his prayer and bowed before the great almighty, Shri Hanuman ji, and then proceeded to his breakfast table. With his mind diverted, it was becoming hard to think clearly. He needed to talk to Dada about it, he knew Daksh had got into something with Raman Ahuja, the gangster, and he also knew the fact that Raman Ahuja wasn't an ally of Rajaswamy Mohan, so it was very probable that Raman Ahuja got his backing from some ministers from the alliance, and if that was the case, Adhiraj could help him, but it might cost Adhiraj his dream, the choice was tough, and he had to make it, really soon. His phone rang, and it was the person Adhiraj wanted to talk to the most, his dada.

"'Hello dada, thank god you called, I needed to talk to you about something." So saying he briefed dada about Daksh, everything from the very start, the informers he had sent to Bhopal, the situation he was in right now . . .

"Well . . . ." Dada finally said after hearing the entire story . . ." I think you should concentrate on your goal right now . . . because, first, you are this close to achieving it, and if you divert your attention now, which will happen, given your emotional connection with the two friends, it might affect the entire plan, and months of preparation would go into the water. Secondly, we don't know anything about Daksh's past, and the people he messed up with, Raman Ahuja is no small man, he is known to have some really strong political backing, and it's not us for sure, so it's either some growing regional party, or alliance itself. And I would advise you not to get in his way. If you want, I can put my best source on him to get the information. I'll try my level best, but I don't make any promises, plus, you need to focus on the job at hand. Remember, Adhiraj, it's what you have wanted all these years . . . something you fought your own father for, something you risked your life for . . . something that you have always wanted . . . you can't risk it for something as uncertain as a long lost friend on your doorstep with some mess he heeds help in cleaning up. Do you understand?"

"Yes dada I do . . . But I really wanted to help him . . . is there a way we can achieve both the things?"

"Well I am going to try . . . As I told you, I'll put someone I really trust after him, but I don't want you. The next step, the final step of our plan is really important, and you need to really focus on that. You are not just going to bring an entire national party down to the ground, but you are also going to rob it off its money and resources. So focus . . . focus on what you want . . . it's for your own good. I have a feeling Ramakant will call you soon."

"Okay dada . . . I'll . . . I'll focus and do what is needed to be done in order to achieve my goal, our goals . . . I'll succeed." Adhiraj said as he hung up. He knew Rajaswamy was right, giving up on your dreams for somebody else was the last thing you would ever want to do as a youngster.

. . . .

Adhiraj made his way through the Delhi traffic, which was hard as always, people rushing to their respective destination, there was no order of any sort, people drove senselessly, not caring about others, just wanting to reach their destinations as fast as possible. Adhiraj certainly missed his driver in such conditions, but right now he had a lot more to worry about. He had received the phone call he had been waiting for, from Ramakant Yadav, the leader of Alliance, one heck of a politician himself, and if it hadn't been for Rajaswamy, under the leadership of Ramakant, Alliance would have ruled the entire country like a dictator. Adhiraj reached the main gate, and the guard let his car in without a question. Adhiraj parked his car, and headed for the main door, were an armed security guard stopped him, and gave him a pat down, once he was sure Adhiraj was clean, he signaled the man standing beside him, a short heighted man, almost as tall as Adhiraj, in his forties, with a moustache, clean shaved shook his hand. It was a firm hand shake Adhiraj noted, he was dressed in Khaki clothes, a simple shirt and a pant, probably Ramakant's assistant, Adhiraj thought to himself. The man introduced himself as Kishanlal, and asked Adhiraj to follow him. Kishanlal took Adhiraj from a side door, avoiding all the hustle and bustle of the main corridor. The side passage led to a small door, which Kishanlal promptly unlocked and let Adhiraj in, there was an old stairwell, and Adhiraj followed Kishanlal to the first floor, where they exited through a similar old wooden gate, and just to the right was the party president's room, which had it's own security guard, which wasn't armed, just holding a thick wooden stick, who saluted Kishanlal and Adhiraj and opened the door for them. Adhiraj made his way into the cabin and the similarity immediately struck him. It was very much like the cabins in BJHP's office, this was just a bit larger, but the design was typically the same. Adhiraj realized that Ramakant wasn't a man of exclusive taste, he relied on the ordinary, 'more focued on his work than the surroundings . . . unlike Rajaswamy . . . 'Adhiraj mused, and sat on the visitor's chair while Kishanlal went and stood beside the main chair, which was facing opposite, with its back towards Adhiraj. Kishanlal and the man on the chair, whose face Adhiraj was yet to see discussed something in hushed voices, and then Kishanlal immediately left. The man then turned the chair and faced Adhiraj, and there was Ramakant Yadav, the man Adhiraj so much wanted to see, and he hadn't changed at all in the years that went by. They were strong rivals for 8 years and neither of them had ever imagined they would be meeting under friendly circumstances. Ramakant Yadav just looked like any other normal politician, a slightly bulged belly, not very tall, in his late fifties, a moustache, white kurta, permanent lines on the forehead with the constant tension, and hair as white as swan. His eyes were deep, and reflected a lot of experience, there was pure lust for power in his very being. Just then they were joined by another member of Alliance, Jayesh Kapadia, who took a seat beside Adhiraj. Adhiraj knew him as well, he was a very reputed MLA, never lost an election from his area and supposedly a very close friend of Ramakant, Jayesh, was, unlike the other politicians in their late fifties, was extremely fit, and still had some grey hair, he too wore white kurta and payjama, and had a very friendly and comforting smile on his clean shaved face.

"Hello Adhiraj how are you?" Jayesh broke the ice between the three people.

""I am okay . . . just got some grudge against Rajaswamy."

"Well that is why we have called you here. We have a small proposal for you."

"What proposal?"

"I'll get straight to the point." This time Ramakant spoke up. "I understand we have a common enemy that we want to bring down. So why not work as friends on this one?"

"I guess you mistook my grudge. My grudge is against Rajaswamy, and you, against BJHP. So we aren't on the same page. Plus we cannot be friends, you know, because friends are those, who have a mutual liking for each other. And honestly, I don't like either of you."

"I know . . . you don't like us, but I have to tell you Mr. Adhiraj Goswamy, I have enormous admiration for you as a politician, and well, if not friends we can work as allies. Plus, as far as the Rajaswamy and BJHP is concerned, what is BJHP without Rajaswamy, Rajeev Sinha and you. Rajeev Sinha has been assassinated, and from what I gather, you and Rajaswamy are sworn enemies now. I mean look at it, he defamed you on the national television, blaming you for all the corrupt activities going on in the BJHP . . . . It isn't fair . . ."

"I know it isn't fair. But I can't do anything about it. Can I?"

"Of course you can . . . we both can help each other . . . do you know why Rajaswamy did this to you?"

"No . . . to be honest, I have no idea . . . And when I get my hands on him, I'll demand all these answers . . ."

"Well Mr. Adhiraj, you don't have to wait that long, I'll give you your answer right now."

"You know???"

"Yes obviously I do. Everybody knows the reason why Rajaswamy wanted to defame you and end your political career."

"What is it?"

"You were growing larger than the BJHP, I mean look at you; you achieved so much in just a small span of 8 years . . . The entire youth of the country started looking up to you, and Rajaswamy feared that you may outgrow his limits of control. Rajaswamy is a devil, he likes to be in control of everything that goes on around in his territory, and when he sees something rising faster than him, he loses his mind and decides to cut him off . . . you are in politics for 8 years son, and Jayesh and I have been dealing with Rajaswamy for over 20 years now. So we know a lot better how he works . . . Look how he treated people in his party . . . as if you are his slaves . . ."

"Why are you telling me all this?"

"I am trying to inspire you to get your revenge . . . I am trying to inspire you to get what you rightfully deserve."

"I see . . . but it's for your own advantage . . . I help you take Rajaswamy down, and then you and Alliance will rule the entire country, and what will I get? I would be left with nothing."

"You are already left with nothing Adhiraj, Rajaswamy ruined your political career, people see you as a corrupt, there is no way you can lead a normal life again. So it's better you become allies with me. I understand we have been in the opposing sides for quite a while now, but take my advice, when you have to choose between two enemies, choose the one who is more personal to you."

"Okay I get it . . . you give me the satisfaction of revenge with Rajaswamy . . . but, after that, what? I need a promising future . . . You will get to rule the country . . . What will I get?"

"Hmmm . . . . I get it. I'll help you start a new life. How's that?"

"I don't want your help with my get away to the new life . . . I need money, I am running short of it now. All my offshore accounts are known to Rajaswamy, and given the current circumstances, the accusations of being a corrupt, I can't risk bringing the money into the country, CBI and the income tax department are keeping a strict eye on my monetary movements."

"Okay . . . I'll give you a 100 crores for the entire job. Half in 2 days, the remaining half, once our deal is completed."

"1000 . . ."

"What???"

"I want 1000 crores . . ."

"Are you out of your mind?"

"You are indirectly buying the whole country Ramakant . . . you could make that kind of money in 6 months . . . you'll have a lot of time to make the profits . . . think wisely . . . it's the best investment scheme you will ever come across . . ."

"You do know how to negotiate . . . I'll give you that . . ."

"Well in my 8 years, I learnt a few tricks of Rajaswamy . . . you yourself admitted I have come so far in such a short time . . . so well yes . . . I have learnt that a good negotiation is neither side leaves with a complete victory or loss. It ends equally, and both the sides leave slightly disappointed."

"Hmm okay . . . well I guess the deal is done . . . You will get the money in 2 days, all cash, Rupee 1000 bills, in stack of 100, cash won't leave a trail."

"Thank you . . ." Adhiraj said, getting up, simultaneously with Ramakant and Jayesh . . . he shook Ramakant's hand, "And because you have been more than co-operative, I'll tell you two things in advance . . . if you want to bring down Rajaswamy, target Rahman Malik, very few people know that he is the brain child of most of Rajaswamy's operations . . . you get him out of the scene, Rajaswamy is broken into half . . . and second, Rahman Malik, is planting evidence to prove that you were the one behind the assassination of Rajeev Sinha. I hope we meet again soon to discuss our plan of action against the two soon." Adhiraj winked . . . "I'll show myself out the way I came in . . . Thank you," and then walked out of the cabin . . .

"Do you trust him?" Ramakant said to Jayesh after Adhiraj left.

"I don't . . . but he holds a lot of grudge against Rajaswamy, and knows a lot of secrets about the party . . . so we will need him for now . . ."

"Yes . . . we need him just for some time . . . but remember, it was your idea to bring him in, and you will be the one who would eliminate him once our job is done."

Jayesh smiled . . . "That goes without saying . . . I'll handle him personally . . . ."

. . . .

CHAPTER 16

4 days later, 3 am, Rahman Malik's bungalow.

THE MAN, COVERED ALL OVER in black, from the mask to the black shoes, neatly scaled the wall on the side of the bungalow. A guard was taking his round around the entire premises of the bungalow. So the man stealthily got behind the guard, and skillfully, without making a noise broke his neck. He then looked around . . . for the other three guards . . . Adhiraj had told him that there are going to be 4 patrolling guards in all, inside the bungalow premises. Ramakant had bought all the policemen outside the bungalow, so the job had become a lot easier . . . and this man was the most skilled assassin money could buy in India . . . Adhiraj had given him the blueprints of the house, told him his entry and exit points, the man just had to follow the directions. And so he did . . . It was a 2 story house, with Rahman's room on the first floor, on the left side of the house. Rahman Malik liked open air, and so his room had a window, but the window was covered with window grating. The assassin didn't seem worried, and he scanned the entire wall, and picked up the points that would help him climb up, he had a back pack, that contained all the necessary things he could need to climb the wall and murder somebody. So he went along with his plan . . . and started scaling the large wall with the help of a high tensile rope that he had latched on a metal bar at the roof. He had practiced all this stuff a thousand times, and now it was a piece of cake for him. On his way up, he took a peek through the window grating, he saw the chief minister sleeping peacefully along with his wife, unaware of his fate . . . the man pulled out his 9 mm, connected the suppressor and smiled at the minister, he had forgotten the number of times he had taken lives . . . it was a lot easier now, his conscious had been silenced once and for all, and taking lives for money seemed fair . . . it was his talent . . . this was the job he was best at and this was the job he loved the most . . . 'Anyways . . .' he knew he couldn't wait for too long in a single place on such missions . . . 3 more security guards were still patrolling around the premises, and his observations had told him that it would be 3 minutes before the guards will question the whereabouts of the missing guard . . . the guard he had killed a some 7 minutes ago . . . the guards took a time of approximately 40 minutes in patrolling one corner, and the place where he was, the distance to the main gate, the check point of the guards was less that 10 minutes . . . and the guards maintained an effective time record of their job. There would be a window of at most 5 minutes before they contact him via the walkie talkie, and when they find no response there, they would come looking for him . . . so in approximately 16-18 minutes . . . there would be a loud alarm and all the authorities would be informed of the security breach in the chief minister's bungalow. He took a careful aim, and shot 5 bullets back to back . . . 3 in the minister and 2 in the wife . . . neutralizing both of them . . . he smiled, put his arms back in their places, and descended down. Now he just had to scale the boundary wall, a police van would be waiting for him, where he would change his clothes, and the policeman would drop him to a taxi stand 2 kms away, from where the man would take a taxi to Bangkok. It won't be till morning that people found out the chief minister and his wife are missing, and by the time, all the authorities would be alerted, he would be lying in a spa in some hotel, attended by a really hot maid who would do anything for the large amount of money he would pay her.

. . . .

The entire country was taken aback by the killing of Rahman Malik . . . . There were emotions of all sorts . . . some people were happy, some people were sad and some people were angry . . . but most of the people were in shock . . . Two of the most important personalities of the country, the prime minister of the country and the chief minister of Delhi were assassinated in a time of 7 days . . . as a result, the constitution gave the president, Rajaswamy Mohan enormous authority, which he sadly accepted. The assassination of the first ever Muslim chief minister in the history of the country's capital just before the re-elections raised more questions . . . some people, especially on the Alliance's side, saw it as an opportunity to ignite people on the basis of religion and spread the word that this was done because the Hindus didn't want to see any Muslim candidate rise to power and the simple people stupidly followed them . . . there were riots between Hindus and Muslims and by the time the day ended . . . the capital was in a complete chaos . . . Rajaswamy was tired as hell . . . the new power and authority had come with a little bit consequence . . . And besides the riot, another thing happened that shook his party to the core . . . The police told the media that when they were searching Rahman Malik's mansion, they found the file of Rajeev Sinha's driver, the prime suspect in the assassination of Rajeev Sinha . . . so it was very probable that Rahman Malik was the one behind Rajeev Sinha's death . . . The opposition leader, Ramakant saw it as an opportunity to further damage the BJHP. He gave a statement to the media that was telecasted on all the news channels in the country, for the entire day . . . .

"It's with great regret I have to say that the future of our country is in the hands of such people . . . We are being ruled by murderers . . . people who can go to any limit to gain power and authority, even murder their colleagues, this was not something that I expected from someone as rational as Rahman Malik, I mean, I personally knew that man once, and he was a man of honor, there is no way he could have done such a thing . . . but as the history says, people follow their leaders . . . and their leader is in a tremendous power right now . . . Who knows where Rajaswamy is leading his men in the pursuit of power . . . I am very sure that further investigation would result in more fingers pointed straight at someone or the other in BJHP. I just hope they realize what they are doing before it is too late. I just want a better future for our country, especially the youths . . . they are the future of our country, and it's our responsibility to provide them with better platform for their careers . . . I sincerely hope that my friends in opposition see this and rather than fighting among themselves, start working for the betterment of the country. I am not going to blow my own horn, or remind you of all the great deeds that me and my men have done for this country, because this is our job, and not a favor on the citizens of this country . . . . Neither am I going to ask for any of your votes . . . you are all smart enough to choose between murderers and silent heroes . . . I don't deny the fact that there are corrupt people in my party, but one thing I am sure of is, there are no murderers in my party . . .

It's high time that people stop fulfilling their lust for power and money at the cost of the common man of the country."

And people listened to him . . . . There was appreciation for Ramakant Yadav and criticism for BJHP, people came out on the streets to support the rallies for Alliance and demonstration against BJHP. If anyone saw the current state of the country, they would believe Alliance would clean sweep BJHP in the re-elections . . . . Everybody except three people . . . who knew exactly what was going on . . .

Rajaswamy smiled as he saw his plan working . . . Ramakant Yadav was overwhelmed and thrilled to the core at the sudden success . . . it had come faster than Ramakant had expected and he was more than overjoyed . . . and also a little overconfident . . . And when a man becomes over confident, and overjoyed with success, he happily lets his guard down, and it is more than easy to strike him . . . just the timing needs to be correct . . . Rajaswamy mused . . . 'Just the timing needs to be correct . . . .'

. . . .

CHAPTER 17

Alliance party office, the following morning.

"Hahaha . . ., well I have to say this Mr. Adhiraj, working with you has been a great pleasure . . ." Ramakant Yadav smiled.

"Likewise . . . I never knew you could run operations so smoothly and you have such well-trained men as your acquaintances . . . Rajaswamy, though has a very good contact list, lacks highly trained personnel."

"Well I am glad that a prominent and respected member of BJHP is impressed by my work."

"Just a minor correction . . . former member of BJHP . . ."

"Hahaha . . . . Yes of course . . . a former member . . . So I guess you are ready for the final plan, to take down Rajaswamy."

"Oh I can't tell you how much I have been waiting for this plan to come into action. What is the plan anyway?"

"Well it's simple . . . Just before the re-elections, say . . . umm . . . somewhere in the next week, we are going to pin the murder of both Rajeev Sinha and Rahman Malik on Rajaswamy, and prove that he did all this for single handed power . . . I have got a few men on the inside on both the police force and the CBI . . . BJHP has lost a lot of support after the turn of recent events . . . and according to you, we have broken the back bone of Rajaswamy, so without the three of you, Rajeev Sinha, Rahman Malik, and you yourself, even if Rajaswamy avoid prison sentence or death sentence, he won't be able to make his way back to the top of the political ladder . . . In the meanwhile, in his absence, which will be for a week or so, it will be easy to break down the remaining of BJHP. Because without a lion, an army of 1000 sheep is useless or, without the brain, even the strongest and most well-built body is useless . . . similarly, without Rajaswamy, BJHP won't stand much of a chance against us . . . There are a few members whom I am particularly targeting, young members, I'll buy them and thus, systematically break down the whole of BJHP."

"I have to tell you this time, that you are a greater mastermind than Rajaswamy. So you are winning the elections this time . . . anyways that doesn't concern me . . . I just want to see BJHP lose and secondly, I want the money you promised . . . I am searching for a way out . . ."

"Absolutely Mr. Adhiraj, you have been fulfilling your side of the bargain extremely well, and so it's my duty to fulfill my side of the bargain as well . . . Here's the address to my farmhouse, as promised you will get half of the money today, and the remaining, after the fall of Rajaswamy, which would most probably, be next week."

"Alright . . . What time???"

"Well its 9 am now . . . how about 5 in the evening?"

"That's fine with me. I guess I'll waiting for you then."

"Yes . . . I won't be there . . . but my men would be definitely there, along with Kishanlal . . . the man who was present here the last time we met . . ."

"Yes I remember him. No worries . . . I understand you are a man of high authority and responsibility, your absence won't matter. I'll call you once I get the money. I hope it is cash."

"It is cash Mr. Adhiraj, you can rest assured. There won't be any money trail of any sort. You can start planning for a safe and secure future . . ."

"Thank you Mr. Ramakant Yadav. I'll be in touch." So saying Adhiraj shook the man's hand and returned through the small door and the stairwell . . . the way he used last time . . . avoiding all the eyes and ears in the Alliance office.

As he disappeared out of the building . . . Kishanlal approached Ramakant . . .

"Sir I thought you were going to double cross him . . ."

"I am . . . I am going to double cross this son of a bitch . . . but not today . . . not till I see Rajaswamy completely destroyed . . . the 20 year rivalry will finally come to an end . . . As far as Adhiraj goes . . . it's a lucky day for the bastard . . . but once Rajaswamy is down . . . Jayesh will personally handle his matter . . . He was right . . . it's the best investment scheme I have ever come across . . . Buying the entire country for a little over 500 crores . . ." So saying Ramakant smiled and slumped back into his chair . . . while Kishanlal laughed and left the room . . . 'Today is a lucky day for this kid . . .' Kishanlal thought . . .

. . . .

Approx. 5 pm, Ramakant's farmhouse, outside the city.

Kishanlal had reached well before time in order to review everything. The farmhouse was set outside the city, in a rare lush green field. The natural beauty was vanishing at an alarming rate in the entire country and this was one rare place in Delhi where you could actually locate some free space. The entire field, of over 20,000 sq. ft. belonged to Ramakant, the beautiful cottage set amidst the greenery belonged to Ramakant, the crops in the field belonged to Ramakant, the cattle grazing in the field belonged to Ramakant. The cottage, though was located in the village, was better than the mansions built in the main city, It had two stories, there was a large swimming pool, a garage large enough to house 5 cars at one time . . . it was painted with rich white color which shone brightly under the open skies . . . Kishanlal was looking at his watch again and again . . . he wanted to get this done with . . . He was accompanied with 3 men, all were bodyguards, to guard the huge amount of money that was waiting outside in a mini truck. Just when he was growing really impatient, he heard the noise of a couple of cars approaching from the distance . . . 'Finally . . . the kid is here . . .' he summoned the three men and decided to meet him at the door itself, give him the money and bid farewell at the gate only. There was no sense in entertaining him as a guest. So he went out, just in time as the two cars stopped at the main gate. One was a police jeep and one was a white ambassador. The policemen immediately got down and pointed their guns at the 4 men emerging from the house. The two men who got down from the ambassador, walked straight up to Kishanlal.

One man, in the mid-forties, medium heighted, totally clean shaved, and a wearing a pair of glasses, showed him a license and identified himself as the commissioner of the Income tax department.

The other man, of a similar age group, a little taller, and better dressed and body built, identified himself as a CBI officer. The income tax officer spoke up,

"We had a strong tip that a few ministers of your party are running black money that was bagged under various scams . . . As a result we are raiding this place. Nobody escapes, we have a warrant to search this place down, and seize whatever we find doubtful."

"You don't know whose farmhouse you are raiding commissioner . . ." Kishanlal scorned at the officer. "I'll screw you. Trust me."

"Hahaha . . . I am not one of those officers whom you can threaten my boy . . . In fact, right now, our department, and CBI, have formed a special team of 60 officers, 20 from anti-corruption department, 20 from CBI, and 20 from Income tax office. They are accompanied by police force, and they are currently raiding 20 different places, all of which belong to different ministers of your party . . . so some free advice . . . don't press me to increase the number of charges on you . . . I hope you co-operate with me and my men . . ."

So saying he signaled the others to move ahead and raid the entire place down, including the truck that was standing in front of the cottage.

Kishanlal felt desperate. He knew he couldn't question the income tax and CBI. So he called and informed Ramakant about this.

Ramakant was furious.

"I want that son of a bitch Adhiraj dead . . . none of his family should survive the attack . . . I want you to take care of him . . . and where the hell is Jayesh . . . I'll tlk to him straightaway."

"Okay . . . ." So saying Kishanlal hung up, and turned his eyes down as he saw the CBI discover the 500 crore in the truck . . .

· · · ·

Same time, Alliance party office.

Ramakant was furious . . . he knew this would terribly harm his party's reputation . . . he had also realized that Adhiraj was still working for Rajaswamy. And he wanted to screw Jayesh . . . it was Jayesh who pressed on involving Adhiraj in the plan . . . and he also realized the fact that Adhiraj and Rajaswamy also wanted to kill Rahman Malik . . . and they had used him to do that . . . Just then his phone rang . . . It was a private number . . .

"Hello . . . whose this?" he answered the phone . . .

"You forgot me so fast? I know you gave a kill order for me and my family . . . but at least remember me . . ." so saying the voice on the other end chuckled . . .

"How??? Adhiraj . . . you son of a bitch . . . I'll find you and I'll kill you . . ."

"Oh I know that . . . We had tapped your phone, and now we have the recording of you giving a kill order for me . . . and it will go public soon . . . by the way don't you switch on the news? There is a big surprise for you . . ." So saying Adhiraj hung up.

Infuriated, Ramakant switched on the news channel and what he saw next almost gave him a heart attack. There was Jayesh . . . addressing the entire nation . . .

"Hello everyone, as one of the most prominent members of the Alliance party, very sadly, I am informing you that Alliance party has become a center of crime and corruption. I can no longer be a part of such a party. Only today I found out about the truths of Rajeev Sinha's and Rahman Malik's murders . . . I have evidences to prove that they were directed by Ramakant Yadav himself . . . the evidences are in my car right now, and from here I am going to go straight to the CBI office, and present them with the entire case . . . these were cold blooded murders just to eliminate competition in the re-elections . . . Just like Anjana Roy, Ramakant Yadav tried to use their murders to bring Rajaswamy down. And I came here before because I know that Ramakant has a lot of people on the inside in CBI, and the evidences can be tampered with . . . and it's my responsibility to let all the Indians know the truth . . . Rajaswamy and BJHP are innocent . . . It's a shame that the murder of people who were as close to them as family, was pinned on them. And today Ramakant wants me to kill the former member of BJHP, the political youth icon, Adhiraj Goswamy. I can't do this anymore. I resign."

So saying he left the news agency. And this news was soon on all the news channels . . . Ramakant lost his mind. He asked his best men to track down Jayesh . . . he knew if anything happened to Jayesh now, all the fingers would be pointed at him . . . but before anyone could track him down, 15 minutes later after this statement . . . another news came and it was another blow to Ramakant and his legacy . . . the car Jayesh was travelling in, had exploded . . . and everything including Jayesh had burned down to ashes . . . And almost at the same time . . . . Another news came in . . . some men opened fire on the Adhiraj's mansion . . . the intense firing had continued for over 10 minutes and there were no survivors in the house . . . two dead bodies were found, a man and a woman, and the police had denied further information to the media . . .

Jayesh switched off his television . . . he had had enough for a day . . . the statement he had given about Rajaswamy earlier that da, came ringing back into his ears . . . 'Even if he avoids the prison sentence or the death sentence, it would ruin his political career . . . .' It had happened . . . only the subject had changed . . . Rajaswamy had won . . . the 20 years of intense rivalry had definitely come to an end . . . but he made his mind . . . though he lost to Rajaswamy, he wouldn't let Adhiraj get the better of him . . . Adhiraj wasn't dead . . . . He knew that . . . Because the person who was going to kill Adhiraj, Jayesh Kapadia, had betrayed him for some reason . . . so he will have to go to his last straw . . . who would kill Adhiraj for him . . . the man who was hidden from the media all along . . . because he was the media himself . . . Daksh Singhvi, Daksh would kill Adhiraj for him . . . he will have to . . . if he wanted to see Charvi alive . . .

. . . .

CHAPTER 18

Present . . . . Near Indira Gandhi International airport.

Adhiraj paced up and down swiftly as he saw several cars and vans and buses going by. Dada told him to meet here. Anjali waited beside the two small bags that was their luggage for the exit. Other than the two small bags, she just had a hand bag that contained her female stuff. Adhiraj looked at his watch for the umpteenth time as he looked at her with a worried face. Dada was always very punctual. And then, finally, he saw the white Mercedes approaching, the car that he was waiting for, and a smile came to his lips, and before he knew, the car stopped. A smile came across Adhiraj's face as the scene from 9 years back replayed. When Rajaswamy Mohan had come in for his rescue after the huge row between Adhiraj and his father. It was the exact replay, nothing had changed in the last 9 years except the hair which used to be black back then . . . Adhiraj with enormous genuine respect saw his mentor, his guide, his godfather, his dada, who wore the unchanging expression, as calm as the sea. Probably one of the most guarded secrets in their party was his relationship with Rajaswamy, and they both preferred to keep it that way. It was all Rajaswamy's game from the very beginning. And their plan had worked out extremely well. Adhiraj and Anjali swiftly moved towards him and touched his feet. He blessed them both and then hugged Adhiraj.

"Thanks a lot son. You have done a great favor on me."

"Dada please, it's you who are giving me my life. You rescued me 9 years ago, made me what I am today, and now you are the one giving me my new life. I should be the one thanking and not you."

Rajaswamy laughed at his reply. And just then they heard the screech of the car. They both turned around to find Daksh, eyes blood red, hair messed up, an angry and hateful expression on his face and a pistol in his hands.

"I'll kill you. You ruined my life you son of a bitch . . ." he shouted, and then there was a bullet shot, then another, then another, and then another . . . . back to back 4 bullets were shot. Adhiraj slowly opened his eyes in terror, he was so shocked that he couldn't tell if the bullets were fired at him or Anjali or Dada. After a couple of moments, he slowly opened his eyes, still in shock, expecting to see all the three people, Anjali, dada and himself bleeding . . . but when he looked at the sight, that horrified him even to his core, Anjali was clung to his shoulder, dada stood there, motionless, and it was Daksh who was bleeding, with 4 large spots of blood clearly visible on his torso, lying face down on the ground. He looked around in horror and saw Prithvi standing there. "You . . . you aren't dead???" He finally managed to utter.

"Yes I am . . . and I guess that's good for you."

"Thanks Prithvi. I'll reward you generously for the great favor you have done to me." Rajaswamy said, in his plain voice.

"I don't want any rewards, I was just on my way to arrest you, and it was god's grace that I got here in time. But I am surprised to see Adhiraj here. After digging for almost 2 months now, I thought I had found out everything that was there to find and known everything I should know. So are you going to tell me the whole story here or in the prison?"

"Well I didn't know you were alive. How about, I tell you my secrets, you tell me yours and then you decide if you want to take us to the prison or not?"

"I guess that sounds alright."

"You want to start?" Rajaswamy asked Prithvi.

"No sir, I guess you should start talking, and that too fast and honest."

"Alright then. It all started 5 years ago. I came to know about a woman, Leelawati Desai, the wife of Vijaykant Desai, was terribly upset and wanted to leave her husband, but Vijaykant wasn't letting it happen. When I dug further into this matter, I found out that the couple had a daughter, who was 17 years old at that time, was brutally raped by her own father, who was in a drunken state. Leelawati tried to stop him but he wouldn't listen, and raped the young girl. The girl went into such a deep shock that she couldn't recover, and died within a week of this incident. Leelawati became so upset and angry that she filed for divorce, but Vijaykant bought all the judges and lawyers to save his political image. I blackmailed Vijaykant with this entire scene and he became ready to do anything that would save his life. So I took Leelawati in, and carved out a revolutionary out of her. She might have been a housewife, but you know, she had the will and drive of a mother seeking justice for her daughter. She had all the anger, I just provided a vent to it. It was me who decided to get you here to ensure Anjana Roy's safety. I was completely unaware of the fact that you three were childhood friends. And you were more than eager to help Adhiraj, who was reluctant at the start, but seeing that there won't be any harm to either of you, he decided to take you in. And then, you know the rest of the story. But tell me, how did Daksh get into all this so deep? And why did he want to kill Adhiraj? I am sure you know the answers to these questions."

"As a matter of fact, you are right. Daksh was forcibly incorporated into Alliance. Raman Ahuja had given him a lot of money to eliminate Anjana Roy. Because they all knew, that she could cause great trouble, though, they didn't know that she was Vijaykant's wife. So they sent Daksh here, as their puppet, to eliminate Anjana Roy, and that's why he was so adamant to kill her. By the way, who killed Rajeev Sinha?"

"Obviously, my men did. He was becoming a problem. He started thinking that because he was the prime minister, everything should go according to him. And plus, I had to vacate the prime minister's seat for my son, Arjun, who is coming tomorrow, and will take part in these elections."

"Hmmm . . . you are such a selfish man you know . . . what about Rahman Malik?"

"Same like Rajeev Sinha . . . he started thinking he was really capable and bigger than the entire party . . . And well . . . I didn't like it . . . So I got him killed too . . . Now Aranya Dixit will take his place."

"Hmmm . . . what about Jayesh Kapadia??? How did you manipulate him, and then why did you kill him when he was finally on your side?"

"Well Jayesh was the one close to Ramakant and was also the easiest one to manipulate . . . I asked him to help me bring Ramakant down, in exchange for the chief minister's seat. And he gladly betrayed his master out of greed. He had to be killed to strengthen the accusations on Ramakant."

"So basically, you ruined so many lives just to get your son on the prime minister's seat and give Adhiraj his fucking writing career."

"Yes you can say that. You might be thinking I am crazy. Let me justify it for you. Prithvi my son, we all have a dream. To be passionate about it is good, but to be obsessed with it, so obsessed that it starts driving you mad, is far better. Because only then, you become an achiever in true sense. Obsessive madness is the first point in the prerequisites of success. And by success I don't mean something as cheap as a competition to be better than someone. Only small, narrow minded people compete, they strive to become the best. But larger people, people with broader mentalities, for them, success is a lot greater than that. For them, success means contentment of heart through the creation and practice of an art of any kind, be it business, be it physics, be it painting, be it writing, or be it politics. And people like this, are very rare, and unfortunately, such rare people are needed by the world. Plus, as his godfather, I have a lot of love and care for Adhiraj and Arjun. I would go to any limits to see these two achieve their goals in life. So if you want to arrest me for that, I surrender. But you know, we could always make a deal."

"Hahaha . . . . You would never change will you? You don't have anything that I want."

"Yes I have, I can free Anjana Roy, and there you go, she would be back to her place, safe and sound. And in return you can let us go."

"Hahaha . . . you really think I am that stupid. You WILL free Anjana Roy, she is your crew, remember. And I have heard, Rajaswamy Mohan, never leaves a loyal man behind. So what else you got?"

"You said I ruined your life. I can return it back to you. Your original place in the Rajasthan police force would be returned to you. In fact, for your efficient work here, you would be promoted two places next week itself. A good cash reward will be given and your name would be nominated for national awards for bravery."

"You know Rajaswamy, you could never understand me. All these things, that you are offering me, mean very little to me. I sincerely wanted to see a corruption free India. And as far as my old life goes, trust me, I can never have it back. Because, back then, I had faith and hope. You broke both of them. Anyways, unlike Adhiraj, friendship means a lot to me. I already killed one best friend today, and am feeling really guilty about that right now, I can't take the guilt of ruining lives of both of my best friends in one single day. I'll let you go Adhiraj. And I don't want any promotion, in fact, today when I'll leave the chowki, I would submit my resignation and quit the forces forever. If you really want to give me anything, just take my resignation, and forget about me, let me live the kind of life I want to."

"Okay, it's our agreement. I'll see that it is fulfilled to your expectations from my side." Rajaswamy forwarded a friendly hand towards Prithvi. Prithvi waved it off, and looked at Adhiraj, who advanced towards him, but was stopped by his gesture.

"It's alright Adhiraj, I know you would be happy wherever you go. And don't worry about Daksh, I'll get someone to call Charvi, and let her know that her husband was killed in a crossfire. I just hope she could take this shock. And I hope we never meet again. Goodbye." So saying Prithvi got into his car, and drove away in the distance, as Adhiraj saw his car disappearing in the distance, with his words ringing in his ears. He knew Prithvi was right, Daksh might have been at fault, but he was somewhere too. After all, he conned his best friends for selfish reasons, friends who trusted him with their lives . . . . He asked Dada to take care of Charvi and then, took Anjali's hand and departed for the airport.

. . . .

EPILOGUE

A couple of hours later . . . .

ADHIRAJ WAS FINALLY ON BOARD for the most anticipated flight of his entire life. A flight to freedom, a flight to happiness, a flight to everything he had ever wanted. Anjali was sleeping peacefully on the seat beside him. The first class barred her from having the comfort of his shoulder. Adhiraj wanted to be happy. His mind was screaming at his heart to smile. The goal was finally a few hours away, and those few hours would pass extremely comfortably, eating swiss chocolates and eating world class food and sleeping. But still, his heart was a wreck. The events of the past 6 months, had left his heart bleeding. The words of Prithvi were still ringing in his ears, the desperation in Daksh's eyes was still blinding his vision, and, even after trying so hard, he just couldn't muster a smile from the bottom of his heart. Other killings like those of income tax officers was nowhere, they were on Rajaswamy's plate. But his friends, his own friends lost everything because of that dream. A simple dream, that had become an obsession, a dream that changed the entire phase of his life, a dream that he was finally going to live, had come at the cost of two lives. Maybe Daksh too was at fault, he could have been honest with them from the start, and surely, Adhiraj would have helped Daksh getting out, maybe along with himself, and the two friends could have lived by the beach with their families ever after. He thought about Charvi, who must now be in a total shock, Charvi's pregnancy was another huge factor. Daksh had confided in him once, and he was so happy, Charvi must have completed her first trimester by now, and she would be heart broken. They trusted him, and he broke it. Complete trust is the heaviest of all elements in life and the hardest to possess, and a broken trust is the deepest and the darkest black spot on the white paper of conscience. Dada had once told him that he should chase his dreams, because of two reasons, first, everybody should chase their dreams, dreams are something that define our very existence, and dreams are something that determine our life after our death. Secondly, according to dada, he had a conscience, and people with conscience cannot survive in the real world. Well there he was . . . He looked at his watch . . . there were still a few hours left before he reached his destination . . . and well . . . . It was the destination he had always wanted to reach.

. . . .

An artist is anyone who dares to dream, who dares to see the world in his one unique light, and then, breaking all the existing conventions, defines his life accordingly. This book is dedicated to all the artists across the globe, who sacrificed a lot of things in their life, just to do justice to the art they were gifted with.

ENGLISH TRANSLATION
OF SELECTED TEXT

"*Arey bhai kaisa hai??? Kahan tha bhai???*"

"*Mai bdiya hu tu bata . . . Tu toh journalist ban gaya yaar . . .*"

"*Haan yaar . . . aur tu, bahut bada police officer . . .*"

"*Kahan yaar . . . bahut kharaab job hai . . . Anyways . . . you know Adhiraj will be here too . . .*"

"*Haan bhai pata hai . . . soch raha tha press conference ke baad mil lunga . . .*"

"*Chal okay . . . Come here only . . . Saath me chal chalenge . . .*"

"*Okay done . . . ye mera card rakh le . . . ek call kr dena mujhe . . .*"

"Hey dude . . . how are you? Where have you been?"

"I am good . . . how are you? I see you have become a reputed journalist."

"Yes man . . . and you joined the forces . . . . Nice . . ."

"Ah it's a bad job man . . . Anyways . . . Adhiraj is going to be here as well . . ."

"Yes I know . . . . I was planning to meet him after the conference."

"Okay . . . come to me . . . we both will go together . . ."

"Alright . . . keep my card . . . . It has my phone number on it . . . call me."

. . . .

"Hey bhagwan . . . mujhe aapne sab kuch diya. Bas isi tarah apni nazar mujhpar banaye rakhna. Mujhe aap pr poora bharosa hai ki mujhe jab jis cheez ki zarurat hogi, aap bina maange hi de denge . . ."

"Lord, you have given me everything, please bless me. I have complete faith in you, and in your deeds . . . Thank you."

. . . .

"Bhaiyo aur beheno . . . . Sabhi ko Rajaswamy ka namaskar . . . hum, puri party ki taraf se, aapko dhanyavaad dete hai ki aapne hum par bharosa kiya aur humein vote dekar aapki seva krne ka mauka diya. Par abhi haal hi mein, kuch galatfehmiyo ka shikaar hokar, Anjana behen humse thodi naraaz ho gyi thi . . . Aur kyoki janta bhi unhi ke samarthan me thi, aur janta ki iccha thi ki hum unki iccha ko maan le, toh humne socha ki kyo na janta ki baat maan li jaaye. Aakhir hum janta k sewak hi hai, janta ka aadesh toh maan na hi padega . . ."

Laadies and gentlemen, a good afternoon to everybody. On behalf of all the members of BJHP, I would like to thank you all for giving us the golden opportunity to serve the nation. For some reason, however, Ms. Anjana does not agree with our administration, and due to misunderstanding, is accusing us of corruption . . . very well . . . we are public servants in true sense and are more than willing to give up power . . .

"Jab ye bill pass hoga, aur aapne jin gine chune mantriyo pr ilzaam lgaya hai, unke saath saath dusre bhrasht netaao ko bhi saza di jayegi. Fir bhale hi who aapke pati hi kyo na ho . . ."

When the law comes into practice, it would be equally applicable to everybody, even if the politician is your husband himself.

"Bhaiyo, beheno, shayad aapko pata nhi hai, hamari Anjana behen, ya mai kahu, Leelawati behen, ke pati aur koi nhi balki alliance party ke neta, Vijaykant Desai hi hai. Khair, is baare me baat chit toh hoti hi rahegi, muhje lgta hai ki Anjana behen ko is shart ke baare me sochne k liye thoda waqt chahiye. Bahut bada faisla hai behen, jitna waqqt chahiye le sakti ho . . . Aaj k liye ye sabha yahi samapt ki jaaye, hum sabhi ko bahut saare dusre kaam bhi hai . . ."

Ladies and gentlemen, it seems like we were being kept in the dark, Anjana Roy, or Ms. Leelawati is none other than the better half of the Alliance minister, Vijaykant Desai. Well we would definitely discuss this further, but for now, I guess we would call it a day, Anjana Roy needs to make some decisions and the rest of us have a lot of work to do."

. . . .